NEV ERM ORE

Nevermore

Wrenn

MONTGOMERY

Nevermore
Copyright © 2019 by Wrenn Montgomery

This is a work of fiction. The names, characters, and
incidents portrayed in this novel are either products of
the author's imagination or used fictitiously.

ISBN: 9781701576186

Cover Design by Kat Savage
Edited by Christina Hart
Formatted by Carrie Gray

First Printing

For both of my nanas—the one who taught me to escape into reading, and the one who taught me stay and fight.

One

Raven

The drink in my hand sloshes over for the third time as a busty blonde bumps into me from behind—*again*. Biting my lip, I count backwards from ten in my head. Patience has never been my strong suit, and patience for drunks is probably at the bottom of my list of attributes.

The guy beside me is a looker from what I can tell, and the blonde's had her sights set on him all night. The "accidental" contact, where she conveniently brushes up against his broad back—also bumping me in the process—is a signature move. Unfortunately for her, he's not paying her a bit of attention. He's been engrossed in his phone for the last hour.

I guess this end of the bar is where the loners hang out. It's the furthest corner away from the band playing eighties music, opposite the bathrooms. Here, there aren't as many people walking by, minimalizing the risk of unwelcome conversation. This end of the bar screams "I'm not here to talk" but girlfriend in the tube top isn't getting it.

The barstools are close together, and I lean over just a smidge so he knows I'm speaking to him without me having to make the effort of turning toward him. Tossing my hair over my shoulder, I keep my voice low and say, "I bet if you let her know you're not interested she'll probably find someone else to take her home."

There. I've done my good deed for the night. Maybe I can save tube top girl from any further embarrassment.

"I'm sorry?" He turns to look at me and my breath hitches.

For a moment I'm stunned by the greenest eyes I've ever seen. Then I snap myself out of it. "The girl behind us. She's bumped into you about twelve times in the last thirty minutes and it's not that crowded in here. She's trying to get your attention, and I can appreciate that but a good portion of my twelve-dollar drink is now on the bar top instead of in my glass."

"I didn't pick up on that. When she comes back, nudge me and I'll end it."

I take him in for the first time, even though he's been sitting beside me for most of the night. Button-down shirt, gray slacks, dress shoes. His hair is short, military style, but I can tell he's got a little product in it, like he's trying to look nice without looking like he cares. He's dressed as if he just came from work, but there's a roughness there. His face holds sharp angles, and his eyes are somehow sad under that striking green.

"You'll end it?" I ask him, grinning. "What are you? An Avenger?"

He chuckles, and his breath smells minty, mixed with the distinct bitterness of the beer he's been sipping all night. "Nope, definitely not an Avenger. Although super powers would be awesome. I just mean if she comes back, I'll let her know I'm not interested." He looks back down at his phone again and turns it face down, then taps the bar and catches the bartender's eye to signal for another beer. "However, you may want to do the same with the guy sitting down there at the corner. He's been checking you out all night."

I don't even glance in the direction he's shrugging toward. I noticed the same guy earlier, and that's partially why I've been trying my best to throw out "I'm unapproachable" vibes.

"Wait, so you don't notice someone *physically* making contact with you over and over, but you noticed the creeper at the end of the bar checking me out?" I try to keep my tone light, but it concerns me that even *he* noticed the guy that's been making me uncomfortable all night.

"Yeah." He rubs his jaw and I notice the stubble that's growing there. "I don't really have an explanation for that. Just felt someone looking at me all night, but every time I glanced up he was staring at you. Just thought you should know." He turns his attention back to his phone before placing it face down again.

Maybe he's a cop. No, surely a cop would notice someone knocking into them constantly. But then again, he seems really distracted by his phone and the lack of whatever he's been waiting for.

A girlfriend? Missed plans? Recent breakup?

This is what I do. I psychoanalyze everyone. I want to know what makes them tick, why they do what they do. People watching is my favorite thing to do, hence why I'm in a bar alone on a Friday night when I have zero desire to be hit on or picked up by anyone.

I glance down at my own phone and see it's almost eleven PM. An early night for most, but I know nothing good happens for a single girl in a bar at this hour, so I gather my things and finish off my drink in one sip.

"You're not going down there, are you?" he asks me. "Tell me you're getting the creepy vibe from him, too."

I pause before I answer, unsure of how or why it would matter to him either way. "Nah, I'm heading out. Nice talking to you, and best of luck with whatever you're waiting on." I nod toward his phone and stand up.

Out of the corner of my eye, I see the creep from the end of the bar mirror my movements. An uneasiness spreads at the base of my spine. I'm probably overreacting, but when I glance over, he's staring right at me, no smile, no hint of an "Oh, I'm just coming over to try to flirt" type vibe. He looks like he's stalking his prey, and while I'm hoping I'm just overthinking it, I slip my hand into my purse to grip my pistol as I start to walk away, providing myself with a little reassurance.

"Let me walk you out. I'm not trying to pick you up, but for my sanity please pretend like you're leaving with me. I don't feel good about that," the handsome stranger before me says, his eyes flying to the creep then back to me.

The vivid green makes my heart race for reasons unknown to me. I don't even like green eyes. Mainly because I don't know where mine came from.

"Okay, yeah. That would probably be best," I hear myself say.

This is so unlike me and it's a little unsettling. I pride myself on being independent and able to take care of myself. I go out like this almost every weekend. Otherwise, I'd stay home and read twenty-four/seven with no human interaction, and my psychology-centered mind needs just enough interaction to assess to keep from going crazy.

Mr. Green Eyes rises with me, putting his hand at the small of my back to make it appear like we're a couple.

Goosebumps break out across my skin under his touch. I could puke at the way I'm reacting to this stranger whose name I don't even know. I mean I've "known" him for about ten minutes and brushed elbows with him, but now I'm leaving the bar with him. Even if it is just a sham, this is not up to par with my usual standards.

We walk forward as one unit, our movements fluid like we've been a couple for years. I can feel the creep's stare as we pass; his disappointment is almost palpable, and a shiver runs through me.

4

It feels like it takes thirty minutes to weed through the people to get to the door. I catch the eye of the tube top girl and see the pout on her face when she realizes her potential catch of the night is leaving with me.

Ten steps later and we're on the sidewalk outside of the bar. The cold air hits me like a dose of reality and I shiver again.

"I'd offer you my jacket but I forgot to grab one before…I just forgot to grab one." He shrugs as he speaks like it doesn't matter to him either way.

I'm dying to know what event made him leave the house without a jacket in the middle of February. He's intriguing me, but I'm going to blame that counselor mindset again.

"Oh it's fine. I just live across the street anyway. Thanks for walking me out." I'm fumbling on my words and again I want to eye-roll at my own damn self.

Yes, he's attractive. His eyes are something out of a sci-fi movie. He's chivalrous but not coming on to me, which is a blessing since he just had to "save" me from a potentially dangerous situation. And he could totally play the damsel in distress card right now if he wanted.

He groans and squeezes the space between his neck and shoulder. "You live across the street?" He glances over his shoulder toward the bar. "Let me walk you over there. I don't know if he's watching and if he sees you going off alone…I'd just rather be safe than sorry. Again, I promise I'm not coming on to you."

Every bone in my body wants to resist and assure him I can walk the five-hundred feet to my home. I hate accepting help from anyone. But a small rational part of me knows he's right, and what harm could it do? Plus, the fact that he doesn't seem too eager to be helping me is actually making it easier to say yes.

I nod and start crossing the street at the corner right down from the bar. I can feel him trailing behind me. He's not walking beside me, and I appreciate that consideration on his behalf.

We approach the bookstore and I pull my keys out of my purse.

"You live in a bookstore?" he asks.

"Above it. I own the bookstore. Makes the commute easy." I keep my answers short, not wanting him to feel obligated to make small talk with me.

"Interesting." He pulls his phone out again and sighs as he shoves it back into his pocket.

I'm still fumbling, only now with the doorknob, which always sticks no matter how much WD-40 I spray on it. "Yeah, super. All right, well thank you again for…this. I mean it. And I have a hard time saying thank you, so…"

My voice trails off as the old oak door finally gives and the smell of old books and ink wafts out with the heat that blasts us. I start to cross the threshold and I feel his hand close around my upper arm.

As I turn to him, his lips crush mine. Soft, giving not taking, and expertly maneuvering around any objection I could throw out.

He kisses me for a good ten seconds. I don't kiss back, but I don't stop him either.

He breaks the kiss and I stare at him, stunned.

"I'm really sorry. Really. Damn. I just promised you I wasn't hitting on you and then kissed you anyway. I just…you looked so…I don't know. Let's blame it on the bookstore," he says.

I know I'm standing here gaping like a fish with my mouth opening and closing, body buzzing, all rational thoughts gone.

What the hell did the bookstore have to do with it?

"I mean, do you want to come inside and see it if it does that much for you?" I ask him.

His eyes lock with mine again and suddenly we're inside the bookstore.

He slams the door closed and throws the lock.

I don't even bother turning on the lights to the main level. His hands are all over me and I can't remember where the light switch is right now anyway. I lead him behind the cashier's desk and push on the false wall that opens up to the staircase.

"Are you the Avenger? Is this your lair?" he asks, managing to gasp the words out in between the collision of our lips.

I chuckle and spin around to take the stairs two at a time before I change my mind about this entire ordeal. I can't even blame this on alcohol. I had one drink, and the majority of it ended up on the bar.

It's those eyes.

I don't even like green eyes.

Wrenn Montgomery

Two

Emmett

I'm not sure what the hell I'm doing.

I was minding my business, nursing my shitty day with a drink. I tried to ignore the gorgeous dark-haired woman next to me while biding the time until I could go back to my apartment.

But when I noticed the guy at the end of the bar staring at her, alarm bells went off in my head—and not the jealous kind. My years of military service and recent law enforcement have taught me to trust my instincts, which of course turned into walking her home. Which now has me following her up the stairs to her apartment, watching her ass bounce with every step she takes.

I have no business being here. I was just trying to kill time while my girlfriend—ahem, e*x-girlfriend*—was getting her shit out of my apartment. And while this does count as passing the time, I probably shouldn't be having a one-night stand with this sexy librarian-esque woman in front of me. But I've started it now, and I'm not a quitter. And damn, she's gorgeous. Plus, I'm still waiting on the text from my neighbor to tell me the coast is clear.

As we reach the top of the stairs, her loft apartment comes into full view. There are some clothes thrown here and there, and it's definitely lived in. I can tell she's not a type A personality, but it's clean and everything seems to have a place, like she's somewhere between a slob and a neat freak. A stark difference from Jenna.

She spins and wraps her arms around my neck, then she begins to walk backwards, leading me toward the king-size bed in the far-right corner.

I reach for her shirt and tug it over her head.

"Wait," she says.

I pause, because if she doesn't want this I'll high tail it out of here. I'm not into pressuring women to do anything they don't want to do. "Do you want to stop?"

She sighs and rolls her eyes. "No, I just need to know your name first. I have standards."

I chuckle and try not to feel as relieved as I do. "Emmett," I say, in between planting kisses on the spot where her shoulder meets her neck. I feel her shudder under my touch.

"Emmett. Nice. Do you want to know mine?"

The way she draws out my name makes me grin. I'll never get tired of this southern accent around here. "If you want to tell me."

She seems to think for a second before answering, "I don't."

I nod and make to continue my work with her belt, pausing and looking up at her to make sure I have permission.

She nods and grabs at mine in response.

This girl isn't like most of the ones I've met in my time here. Of course, I've been holed up with Jenna for the last six months and haven't exactly been paying attention to the opposite sex, but I've had my fair share of girlfriends and one-night stands and this woman is an enigma.

Her jeans are down around her ankles now and I see she's wearing navy boy-shorts. They're cute, and they cup her ass nicely, but they don't say "I'm trying to get laid tonight" the way a black thong does. It makes me wonder why she was in the bar alone on a Friday night, but I guarantee this closed book isn't going to tell me anything, and who am I to ask? We both know what this is.

She kicks her jeans off and unhooks her bra, letting it fall to the floor, revealing her perfect breasts.

I try not to stare but I can't keep my hands away. The second I place one of her nipples between my thumb and forefinger her head rolls back and a moan escapes her lips, sending a shock wave straight to my cock.

She pushes my pants down so I'm standing in my boxers.

Her eyes gleam as she reaches out and wraps her fist around me through the thin material. "Nice."

I push her backwards gently so that she falls onto the bed behind her, her dark hair a stark contrast against the white sheets. I'm hovering above her, both of us down to just our underwear. I press my pelvis against hers so she can feel how hard I am, and I kiss down her neck toward her chest.

Her breath quickens as she reaches inside the waistband of my boxers and shimmies out of her panties.

I yank my boxers down and lunge for my wallet to grab the gold packet inside. "Last chance. If you don't want to do this..."

Another eye-roll. "Put the condom on and come on. Making me wait isn't doing you any favors."

"Favors, huh?" I roll the condom up the length of me and look down at her.

Thighs open for me to see all of her; she's not shy at all. There's something about a woman with confidence that drives me wild. Her hair is fanned across the pillow above her head and her eyes are hooded. Full pink lips are curved into the perfect pout, while also looking like they're about two seconds from cussing me out and calling this whole thing off.

I drive into her in one thrust and temporarily lose myself.

Holy shit.

Her deep intake of breath tells me she's feeling the same magic I am, and when she starts to buck her hips under me I have to take a deep breath. Coming in thirty seconds would be an embarrassing first for me and I want her to enjoy this.

Get out of your head, Emmett. Act like you've done this before. You're not some sixteen-year-old virgin.

Her moans grow louder with every thrust and she wraps her legs around my back, digging her heels into my hips to drive me closer and deeper. I'm not going to last much longer and I'm not selfish.

I pull out of her and spin her onto her stomach. Pulling her hips up, I enter her from behind. The squeak she lets out makes me grin. She may act like a confident sex goddess, but something tells me she's not as experienced as she's leading me to believe.

I press my chest against her back and wrap my arm around her, pressing my fingers into her swollen clit while I piston in and out of her. I feel her clenching up, her head thrown back to my shoulder, arms shaking, before she suddenly explodes with a yell.

She collapses onto her belly and I pull out again, rolling her onto her back and entering her as quickly as possible. The sounds she's making alone could make me come right here and now and I really want to be inside her when that happens.

A few more pumps, her hands tugging at my hair, and her content mews are all I can take and then I'm spent. I rest my forehead against hers, getting myself together. That was unlike anything I've ever experienced, and I'm pretty damn experienced.

I open my eyes to find her staring wide eyed at me. "You okay?" I ask.

Nevermore

She turns her head to the side, avoiding eye contact as she shoves me off of her and starts to stand up. "Yep, fine and dandy. That was nice. You're welcome to use the shower before you leave."

And just like that she's walking back down the staircase, still naked as the day she came.

Wrenn Montgomery

Three

Raven

Holy shit. Holy shit. Holy shit.
What did I just do?
Did I seriously just let a man I've never met walk me home from the bar and have his way with me? And then I got up and left him in my apartment? Alone?

I don't even know his last name, but at least I have his first.

I keep an old pair of sweats downstairs for when I'm binding books and don't want to get glue on my good clothes. So I go to the back to grab them and start pulling them on, my body still tingling from five minutes ago.

I have never finished like that during sex. On my own, sure. Which is mostly what happens around here these days. In fact, I think I've only brought three guys home since moving into the bookstore two years ago. I usually go to their places, but if I'm being honest even that has been few and far between.

I wouldn't say I'm promiscuous by any means. I haven't had a serious boyfriend since Landry, but I will occasionally go home with someone after a night out with the girls or on my own. I don't do dating apps. Well, I don't do dating in general. So the one-night stand kind of deal is the perfect arrangement for me right now. I just don't do it as often as I should apparently, or sex with Emmett the mystery man would not have affected me like it has.

I hear him coming down the stairs and fight the urge to duck down behind one of the bookcases in front of me. Conveniently, it's the poetry aisle.

Man up, Raven. You did the deed and now it's over. No need for it to be awkward.

His bare feet come into view first, followed by his shapely calves and then his thick muscular thighs, the tops of which are covered by his black boxers. He's still shirtless and I take this half a second to ogle his defined abs and perfect amount of chest hair before his face comes into view. Those electric green eyes scan the room before settling on me and narrowing.

Shit.

"Why did you take off like that?" His voice is soft, not accusatory, which puts me at ease, but I don't want him getting the wrong idea.

"I wasn't aware this was a thing. Aren't you leaving? Figured I'd save us the awkward conversation and yet, here we are."

He smirks. "You always been such a hard-ass?"

His question catches me off guard and I smirk back. *If he only knew.*

"Nope, not always," I say. "Do you want a prize or something? An award? Nice dick, thanks a lot for walking me home, here's a cookie for your troubles?"

"You don't have to be so crass." His eyes catch mine again and I feel my façade slipping.

Why is he so attractive?

"Why the contacts?" I blurt out, anything to take the heat off of me.

"What?" Those green eyes narrow into squints, and he looks at me like I'm insane.

"Your eyes. No one's eyes are that green."

"These are my real eyes, gorgeous. Promise."

My head tilts and I don't believe him. "Gorgeous? Really? How cliché."

"Well, you didn't want to tell me your name, and you are gorgeous. What would you rather me call you?"

"Raven. My name is Raven," I almost spit at him.

Why I'm so offended suddenly, I have no clue. Running a mental self-check, I try to place my anger. He's been nothing but nice to me.

Why am I acting like this?

Because I feel seen, and I don't like to be seen.

"Raven. Nice. Fits you." His eyes gleam as he crosses the old wooden floors to reach me, running his hands through my black hair once he does. "Can you come back to bed with me? I can leave if you want, but I'd like to stay a little longer if you'll have me."

My gut reaction is to say no. But I don't. "Sure, okay, but don't get any ideas. This is still a one-time thing. So you've got the rest of tonight and then this is done. Deal?"

He chuckles and grabs my hand, leading me back toward the staircase. "I really do want to know why you have a hidden staircase, though. That's a first for me."

I notice he doesn't say deal.

"A few reasons. So the customers don't see a staircase and think there's a second floor of the store for them to explore. So I can hide away at the end of the day, or during the middle if I need a break. And maybe a little so that I can feel like a superhero with a lair."

"Knew it."

I roll my eyes again and head for the kitchenette while he climbs back into my bed. I need a distraction and a second to sort out my feelings, before I consider breaking my double-dipping rule.

I am not sleeping with him again.

"You want a snack?" I ask him.

"Sure. I could use something to get my energy levels back up." He smiles at the end, and I'd normally roll my eyes at a high-school-level joke like that, but I catch myself grinning.

"Bacon it is," I say.

"Bacon? At midnight?"

"When else do you eat bacon?" I counter.

"Good point."

My kitchen area is small, but I love it. White tile, a big window above the sink so I can look out at the street below, and gray slab countertops that I poured myself when I moved in and renovated the loft area.

"Do you want it crispy?" I yell to him.

"The crispier the better. Burn it."

"No," I chuff. "You're a monster."

I finish cooking the entire pound of bacon and pile it onto a plate, some crispier than others.

He's turned the TV on and ESPN is scrolling through the highlights, exactly where it was when I turned it off earlier.

"You watch ESPN? Or is there a boyfriend I should know about it?" His tone is light, so I don't take offense to the sexist comment.

"Nope, no boyfriend. I like sports. Mostly football, but I can handle any of them. Except golf. I draw the line there."

"Me too. Also not too fond of hockey but I can see the hype. Getting to smash into your opponent without getting a foul called on you probably has its benefits."

I nod in agreement.

We sit in silence for the next half hour, watching the highlights from the Superbowl last weekend as we make our way through the pile of bacon.

When we're finished, I let out a yawn and stretch, thinking he'll surely get the hint and start getting dressed to leave. Instead, he rolls closer to me and pulls me into his side.

What the hell?

I thought most guys wanted a reason to head out after picking up a random girl in a bar. Why is he sticking around like this? Psychoanalyze in three, two, one...

"Soooo, what are we doing?" I can't help it. I can't leave good enough alone.

"Uh, well, we're currently lying in your bed, listening to the sound of sports highlights, smelling like bacon grease, and enjoying each other's company."

"So...you're staying?" I ask him.

"If that's all right with you? Or I can leave." With the last part of his sentence he presses his hips into mine again and I feel his growing hardness.

As much as I want to kick him out, I also sort of want to see if earlier was a fluke or if he's always that good in bed.

I turn to him and let him kiss me, running my hands against the stubble on his face and letting his hands roam wherever they want to. I'm still wearing my downstairs clothes, which means I'll have to remember to take them back down tomorrow morning, but the sweatpants are giving him easier access and I'm not wearing any underwear thanks to my hasty escape earlier.

"You can stay." I whisper it, because whispers aren't as serious as words said aloud and therefore can't be held against me later.

Right?

An hour later, I'm exhausted.

He gave me two more orgasms and now he's snoring softly behind me, spooning me.

He's definitely good in bed, I'll give him that.

And that's the *only* reason I'm letting him sleep in my bed tonight.

In the morning, he better be gone before the store opens, and hopefully I can forget about this whole thing.

Hopefully I still want to.

Wrenn Montgomery

Four

Emmett

The weight of a heavy quilt and the smell of old books remind me that I'm not in my apartment before my eyes even open. I reach across the bed searching for body heat and find none.

She's already up for the day?

The sun isn't even all the way up yet.

I've always been an early riser, blame it on my time in the Marines or on my father who had me up and ready at six AM, even in the summer. Sleeping in is a waste of precious daylight, but I would be willing to waste a few more hours if it meant I was wrapped around Raven in her bed.

I'd woken up a few times during the night to find her limbs entwined with mine. She tries to act like she has this tough exterior, but body language says a lot, even while sleeping.

I sit up and look around, taking in her apartment again. Everything is neutral; there's hardly any color. A gray throw blanket hangs off the end of the couch, and there's a basket of cream blankets in front of the old fireplace. Her couches are a light gray fabric, and the walls are painted a charcoal color. The appliances are stainless steel. Even the cabinets in her kitchenette area are a shade of the hue.

The only color that I can see are the pots of plants and greenery that seem to line every surface. The large windowsill and bench seat are full of them. There are hanging baskets in the windows with vines spilling out of the pots and trailing down toward the floor. On several of the walls there are giant book covers blown up in black and white. I wonder if they're her favorites. Even though I don't know her at all, I can tell her space fits her perfectly and I'm sure she decorated every inch of it herself.

The shower is running, and I can see steam rolling out from under the door that leads to the bathroom—the only part of the apartment that's closed off. I consider getting up and joining her, but the water shuts off, so I watch the rest of the sunrise through her large picture window before she eventually comes out. Wrapped in a towel, hair wet and hanging in loose waves down her back, I can see water droplets on her skin that she didn't dry off thoroughly. I suppress the desire to go lick them off of her and clear my throat instead.

She jumps a little and spins around, eyes narrowing when she sees me. "What are you still doing here?"

"Oh hey. Good morning to you too, gorgeous."

"Raven," she corrects, not letting the nickname slide. "Seriously, are you ever leaving? Or are you moving in? If so, I'll expect rent on the first of every month. We can prorate this month since we're two weeks in already."

I chuckle and slide off of her bed. Her eyes dip down and I realize I'm still naked, with some nice morning wood going for me, which isn't going away with her standing in front of me the way she is. "I'm sorry. I didn't intend to outstay my welcome. Hell, I didn't mean to stay at all. I'm leaving now. I'll use your bathroom so you can get dressed in peace."

She nods and heads over to her armoire.

I watch her ass sway as she walks, and I head into the bathroom before I go back on my word. Last night I only came in here once, and I didn't turn the light on because I didn't want to wake her. Now I see that it's easily the grandest part of her place. It's at least half the size of the main apartment, with a matching large picture window. There's a massive clawfoot tub in the center, and a shower built for two off to the side. White tile everywhere, double sinks, and a vanity with makeup scattered all over the counter. Gray towels and accents, of course, and even more plants. It smells faintly like apples—must be her shampoo.

I make quick work of using the toilet and washing my face off at the sink that looks like it goes unused. I wait a few more minutes before coming out, hoping to give her enough time to be dressed.

I emerge from the bathroom and she's nowhere to be seen. My clothes are folded neatly on the end of her bed, and there's a note in her tall skinny handwriting.

Emmett,

Thanks for last night. Seriously. Sorry I'm such a bitch. Lock the door when you leave.

Raven.

She's not here. *She seriously left her own apartment without saying goodbye?*

That seems a little cowardly for the girl who seems to stare everything in the eye and take it head on.

Also, who puts a period after their name?

I head downstairs and sure enough, she's gone. I do as she asked and lock the door of the storefront on my way out, but not before scrawling my number at the bottom of the note she left. A little part of me is hoping she calls, but I know she won't. I'll have to keep myself from turning into a stalker and coming by the bookstore.

Something tells me she won't be as easy to forget as I hope she is.

Wrenn Montgomery

Five

Raven

I flew out of the bookstore as fast as I could.

At least I left a note, right?

And I was running late. That's my excuse for my behavior. It has nothing to do with the butterflies Emmett gave me all night, or how ridiculously comfortable it felt to wake up in his arms this morning. I glance down at my Apple watch—it's seven after eight.

Elli is going to kill me.

The coffee shop we meet at every Saturday morning is one block away from my bookstore so there's no reason for me to be late, and she will for sure point it out. I jog past the florist shop on the corner and almost run into a lady holding a dozen daffodils.

It's a miracle Elli hasn't called me yet. Actually, it's unusual. Normally she'd be calling me one minute past eight, asking why I had the audacity to keep her waiting. I love my best friend. We'd bonded over our mutual inherent bitchiness. However, that's about where our similarities end.

Elliott—or Elli for short—is petite, with proportionate curves and a curt blonde bob that is angled so sharp it could probably cut you. I'm tall, willowy, and my black hair flows down my back, hence my name. Elli is a lawyer, a bona fide ball buster, and she takes zero shit. She's a little materialistic and lives in a nice modern penthouse suite uptown. I'm a licensed counselor who opened a bookstore to take a break from seeing patients, and then moved in to the loft above it.

I'd say I don't take any shit either, but I let a stranger convince me to let him stay the night, so...

But the sex was great, and I avoided the awkward morning after conversation, so who's the real winner here?

I round the next corner and enter the coffee shop. It's a cute little shop with a lot of character. I head straight to our corner but stop short when I see our normal table is empty.

What the hell?

I approach the counter while pulling out my cell and flagging down Missy, the owner. She's a short round woman who loves coffee and baked goods so much that she couldn't stand the corporate world any longer and sold everything she had to buy this historic shop downtown.

"Missy, has Elli been in this morning?"

"No, I was just getting ready to call you. It's unlike her. You haven't heard from her?" Missy's face crinkles with worry lines and I get a sinking feeling in my gut.

I shake my head and check my phone, having no missed calls or texts from Elli. I dial her number four times in a row while I stand at the counter, but it keeps going straight to voicemail. "She isn't answering." I bite my lip, trying to decide if I'm overreacting, but I know I'm not. "I'm going to head over to her apartment and check on her. Can you have Jason run down and open the store for me at ten? Just in case I'm not back in time?"

"Sure, honey. I'll have him go down now and start opening up." Missy yells over her shoulder for her husband and he appears instantly.

They've been married for twenty years and they're almost like an aunt and uncle to me. We met in a small business owners' council for the city and they took me under their wing. They're always there when I'm in a pinch and need help covering the store, since I only have two full-time employees who don't come in until noon, if they come in at all. College students, always super dependable.

"Thank you, guys. I'll call you and let you know that she's all right when I get there. She probably just slept in…"

My voice trails off because we all know Elliott James hasn't overslept a day in her life.

Missy nods at me encouragingly but I see the worry all over her face and it does nothing to ease the panic growing in my chest.

I run back to the bookstore and see that Emmett is long gone, but he left his number on the bottom of my note. Big block numbers. *Cute.*

I snatch the keys off the hook by the door and run around back to jump in my car. It's about a ten-minute drive uptown to where Elli's penthouse is. I don't even turn the radio on, which is unheard of for me. I keep calling her the entire way, but it continues going to voicemail.

I get there in six minutes, throw my keys at the valet, and run up to the doorman. "Has Elli come downstairs this morning, Albert?"

He's the sweetest old man who always has peppermints in his coat pocket, and he reminds me of everyone's favorite grandpa. He's worrying his lip and pacing a little when he sees me. To see him concerned only makes me surer that something is really wrong.

"No, ma'am. The night doorman told me earlier that she went upstairs with a fellow last night around two AM, but he came down shortly after and she hasn't." He moves past to let me in to the building.

I sprint to the elevators and enter the passcode to go up to the top floor, trying not to slide across the marble floors. Elli has the level to herself. She's done well with one of the law firms here in town, becoming the first woman there to make partner. No one ever doubted she would. She's the hardest worker I know.

I see my reflection in the gold doors in front of me. My hair is a mess, frayed, just as my nerves are right now. I didn't have time to put makeup on in my haste to escape Emmett and I'm wearing a large hoodie with my favorite ripped jeans. I look panicked. My face is as white as a sheet. The doors can't open fast enough.

The elevator dings as the doors open to her foyer and immediately my hair stands on end. Something definitely isn't right. Her purse is on the table outside of her door, where she would never leave it. One heel is against the wall and the other is halfway between the elevator and her door like they were flung off, or she kicked them off.

Elli has a place for everything. She would never leave her shoes like this, even if she was drunk.

I get my phone out and call downstairs to Albert as I make my way through the foyer to her front door. "Albert, have the front desk call nine-one-one and stay on the phone with me."

I pull my pistol out of my purse, thanking God that I grabbed it before bolting out of the apartment, and I tentatively call out for her.

I hear a groan and rush into her living room.

It's chaos. Everything is turned over—couch cushions off the couch, lamp broken on the floor, blood on the pristine white carpet. My stomach flips and I scream for Albert to get upstairs now.

I call Elli's name again and sprint into her master bedroom. She's tied to her bed in just her bra and panties, covered with blood, face swollen.

"Oh my God. Elli!" I rush to her side and start untying the ropes that are binding her to the bed frame. "Can you hear me? It's Raven. Try to open your eyes. I'm here. It's all right."

Her eyes are swollen shut and her lip is busted. She's trying to make words but nothing is coming out.

"Shh, it's okay. Don't talk. Everything is okay. Albert called nine-one-one. We're going to get you all fixed up." I know I'm talking gibberish, trying not to let the rage that's filling me spill out and keep me from being able to comfort her.

Albert bursts into the room and draws a deep breath.

"Help me get these ties off of her!" I tell him.

We undo the ropes and as soon as she's free, Elli curls into a ball and starts sobbing. I lie with her and hold her, swallowing my own tears. For the next five minutes we just lie that way, me gently rubbing her hair and telling her it's going to be okay and trying to check her over for any more injuries, and her sobbing like a broken woman, making my heart break into a thousand pieces.

The cops show up quickly and rush in. I step back to allow her to be evaluated, and the paramedics clean her up as best as they can before taking her downstairs to transport her to the local medical center. The crime scene investigation unit pulls up as Elli is loaded into the ambulance.

I hop in my car and follow behind them, calling Missy on the way to tell her what's going on and then trying my best to calm her hysterics.

My mind is running a million miles a minute. The night doorman had seen the man. She has security cameras. Surely not all of that blood is hers. There's got to be DNA.

We're going to find him. I'm going to kill him. Please, please, whatever god is listening, please don't let there be any serious damage.

My psychology side is going through all the counseling she's going to need and how to best handle her recovery She's so strong-willed and hard-headed. This is not going to break her.

We're going to get through it—even if I have to pull her through it myself.

Six

Emmett

I take the stairs to the third floor of my apartment building. It's older and it's not the nicest, but it's clean and close to the station. A lot of the single officers live here for that reason. I don't usually take the stairs, but I hate making small talk with my neighbors and I could use the exercise to burn off some frustration.

I can't believe she just left like that. I know I should just chalk it up to a one-night stand and let it go, but there was something about her.

I check my watch as I unlock my apartment door. I've got twenty minutes to shower and put on my uniform before I need to leave to be at work by nine. Weirdest thing about small towns, the cops' workdays start at nine like everyone else's. Nine to five. I just switched back to day-shift after a long stunt on night-shift, thanks to my partner sleeping with my girlfriend. Classic. He told me he was running home for his lunch break all those nights, but he was really running to *my* home to be with *my* girlfriend. My dumb ass was too busy trying to befriend our seniors at the station, so I never came home on breaks.

Yesterday I had taken the day off to go visit my brother, but halfway there I got a voicemail from Everette saying he had barracks duty so I went back home instead. Imagine my surprise when I unlocked my door to hear a distinctive moan coming from my bedroom. I headed toward it, then opened the door to find Alex balls deep in Jenna, who immediately started crying and apologizing.

It stung a little that Alex would do that, him being my partner and all. But if I'm being honest, I wasn't that attached to Jenna. I mean, sure, I liked her. The sex was decent. She could cook. My house was always spotless because she was such a neat freak. And while she didn't technically live with me, she pretty much did, even staying on the nights I was working so that I could "come home to a clean house and nice meal"—her words, not mine. In reality, she was probably staying to be closer to the station for when Alex took his breaks and snuck over here.

This is my first time back to the apartment after catching them yesterday, and it looks like she didn't take anything that wasn't hers—*thank God*. There's a note on my coffee table that I ball up and throw away without reading. I don't care enough about what she has to say to waste my time reading it.

I hit the shower and let the water wash away my thoughts of Jenna along with the remnants of last night. My mind instantly goes to Raven and the way she bit my shoulder and actually left a mark, but I couldn't care less. The sex was incredible. I've got to find a way to see her again. I jump out of the shower and shave the stubble off that always comes back with a vengeance before my next shift.

Fifteen minutes later my face is smooth, my slacks and dress shirt are pressed and neat as a pin, and I'm heading out the door. I'm thankful for the short walk to the station. I don't like to waste time, and a long commute is a waste of time. The walk takes me about five minutes and I feel a sense of pride wash over me as I take in the large stone building.

I didn't plan on being a cop, but the sense of belonging is as close to the Marine Corps as I'm going to get. As I walk in the side entrance I hear my name being called from the second-floor balcony.

My new partner—Monica Tropp—is flagging me down and hauling ass down the flight of stairs in front of me. "Detective Fisher, hate to be the bearer of bad news, but we've got to roll out. Rape victim over at Penn Memorial."

Fuck.

After murders, rape cases are the worst. I have to get into a special kind of head space to investigate them. The broken women, the mental anguish they're going through. Then there's interrogating the suspects who have no respect for women and have committed the ultimate crime against them with no remorse. Makes me want to puke just thinking about it, but I know this is my job and this is why I do what I do. We put those fuckers behind bars.

"All right, let's go." I snatch the keys out of the air as she tosses them to me and we're off.

On the way over to the hospital, she briefs me with the details that we know. "The victim is Elliott James, a prominent lawyer in town. She's twenty-six, lives alone in the penthouse apartment of a new building uptown. She went out for drinks last night with coworkers, and at the end of the night she took a guy home from the bar. The doorman is the only person who's been interviewed so far. He saw them come in around one forty-five in the morning, and Miss James seemed to have been drinking but was able to walk in on her own. She wasn't slurring her words and seemed to be of sound mind to make her own decisions, so the doorman wasn't alarmed by the situation. About an hour later, the companion that had entered the penthouse with Miss James left alone and didn't seem to be out of sorts. When Miss James didn't meet her best friend for coffee this morning, the friend became concerned and went to check on her at her apartment. She found Miss James bound to her bed with nylon ropes. There appeared to have been a struggle, and not all of the blood at the apartment was Miss James'. The crime scene unit is still at the apartment now collecting evidence."

"Okay, so we should have DNA. The doorman sounds like a good witness. Have we checked on security camera footage from the penthouse?" I ask her.

"Yes, the doorman sent it over right before you got here. There isn't a good facial shot but we can definitely tell defining details of body type. White male, probably around thirty, dark blond hair, average build."

"We need to get a list of coworkers she was with last night and interview them. Maybe they saw who she left with or met him before they all split up for the night," I say.

"She's awake and talking so hopefully she can provide us with a list. The officers that have stayed with her have advised us to be aware of the best friend, who's a little shaken up and extremely protective of Miss James. Apparently she's bitten the head off of many an officer this morning." She chuckles a little there at the end, probably picturing our fellow officers getting an ass chewing from some ritzy upper-class best friend.

Wonderful. I mean, don't get me wrong, I understand being protective of your best friend. And I'm sure it was a very stressful and traumatic situation to walk in to. But we need all the help we can get with this, not a best friend interfering and holding up the investigation.

It helps to have Monica along. A woman can often sympathize with victims and make them feel safer. Plus, Monica is a damn good detective. Another benefit of Alex fucking me over by literally fucking Jenna.

We reach the hospital and show our badges at the front desk, where they direct us to the third floor where the victim is being treated. She's not in ICU, so that's a good sign.

Nevermore

We step off the elevator and round the corner to room three-o-eight. Monica knocks twice and enters when someone mumbles for us to come in.

As soon as I step inside the door I swear I can sense her.

My eyes scan the room, and there, sitting at her best friend's bedside, is Raven.

Wrenn Montgomery

Seven

Raven

About thirty minutes ago, Elli finally calmed down enough to stop sobbing. I can tell that she's deep inside her head right now. I'm pretty sure my heart is lying somewhere on the floor beneath this chair I've been sitting in for the last hour. I'm not super religious, but I think I've prayed more this morning than I have in two years.

I'm so glad that she's physically okay. They think she was raped and may have some internal injuries and a concussion, but it could have been so much worse. He could have killed her. I know how strong she is, though, and I know she's going to get through this. She's got a determined look in her eye already. As soon as her physical body is healed, we'll start working on her spirit.

"I should have known better, Rave. I don't know what I was thinking. I never take guys back to my place," Elli says.

"Don't you dare blame yourself, not even for one second. Do you hear me? None of this is your fault. He's a monster, and we're going to find him," I tell her.

"I know. I know we will."

There are two soft knocks at the door and Elli tells the visitor to come on in.

Only, it's not a visitor, it's a detective. Beautiful ebony skin and dark hair slicked back into a bun. Her face is feminine but you can tell she's all business. Her lavender button-down shirt complements her perfectly. Light gray dress pants and sharp black heels complete the look. Her eyes find Elli and I don't see sympathy wash over them.

I'm grateful for that. Elli is not the type who wants to play up being the victim and she damn sure won't take anyone's pity. As the detective shuffles in I realize she's not alone. I catch one broad shoulder followed by another and a feeling of familiarity comes over me.

Emmett strolls in, stopping dead when he scans the room and his eyes land on me.

Shit.

I almost laugh out loud.

Of fucking course he's the detective investigating this. Perfect.

I don't have time to dance around whatever morning-after awkwardness is about to go down, so I avert my eyes. It's hard to, though. He looks amazing. I can tell he just shaved, and he looks more rested than he did last night.

He turns to Elli and says, "I'm Detective Fisher, this is Detective Tropp. We're here to take your statement and see if we can get some information about last night."

Elli nods at them and takes a deep breath.

"Do you feel like you can speak with us right now, or should we come back later?" he asks.

"I'm ready now." Elli's voice is defiant and strong.

I'm so proud of her in this moment, but I know that the strong front she's putting up is going to slip sooner or later, and I'll be here with her when it does.

"Perfect, are you okay with your friend staying?" He motions over to me without looking in my direction, like he has no idea who I am, and I guess he really doesn't.

It stings a little and I want to roll my eyes at myself.

Isn't that what I'm doing to him, too?

I'm glad he's being a professional and doing his job right now. We can talk later.

Maybe.

"Raven," Elli says. "This is my best friend, Raven Jackson. And yes, I'd be more comfortable if she stayed."

I'm grateful, because I want to know what happened but I didn't want to ask her to go through it with me this morning knowing she'd have to do it all over again when the cops came.

"Okay, great." He sits down in a chair at the foot of her bed and Detective Tropp takes her side opposite of me.

The female detective pulls out a notepad and looks at Elli with understanding in her eyes. "Let's just start at the beginning, and if you get uncomfortable at any time we can stop, all right?"

Elli nods.

"Which bar did you go to for drinks last night, and whom did you meet there?"

Detective Tropp is asking the questions, probably a technique taught in school because victims are more susceptible to open up to the same sex. I wonder if this is his partner or if they sent her along since this is a rape case.

"My coworkers, Beth, Lauren, and River. We went to *Drinks on Main* around eleven thirty after having dinner at *The Red Umbrella*."

My forehead gets prickly. *Drinks on Main* is where Emmett and I met last night. I didn't know Elli was going there or I would've stayed longer.

"Lauren and Beth left around midnight. They have kids and they don't ever stay out late with us when we have our girls' nights. River and I stayed until a little after one. She was leaving with a guy she knew through her sister, and I had been dancing with a guy most of the night. He told me his name was Brent, but I don't think that was his real name." She tries to repress a shudder at the end of her sentence, while picking at the white blanket covering her legs as she talks.

"Can you describe him for us? What he looked like, what he was wearing. If he said anything abnormal."

"He was tall, dirty blond hair, wide nose, handsome but not overly so. I'd say he was a decent seven out of ten. Probably six-foot-one, two-hundred pounds or so. I don't remember him saying anything abnormal. He was sweet, but maybe a little pushy on the dance floor. He did mention coming home with me a few times and I laughed it off. He didn't act offended, but he was persistent. I'd only had a few drinks so I thought I was fine. He offered to drive me home anyway and I agreed. I remember getting in the elevator, but that's it. I don't remember being in the apartment at all. Nothing until seeing Raven this morning and the ambulance ride over here. He told me something about putting me to bed in the elevator, and I remember laughing, thinking it was ridiculous because I wasn't drunk and didn't need to be put to bed. But that's the last thing I remember."

"We're waiting for the blood test results to come back to see if she's been drugged," I say, speaking up for the first time, my voice shaky.

Emmett looks my way for half a second, something flashing in his eyes, and then turns his attention back to Elli.

I know we're both thinking the same thing. The man she described sounds just like the creep from the bar last night. I feel sick to my stomach, and guilt is creeping up my spine. Logically, I know it's not my fault this happened to her. But the thought that it could have been me, had Emmett not been there, makes me feel horrible that it was Elliott instead, and that I wasn't there to save her from what happened.

"We'll need the contact information of the ladies that were with you last night. Maybe one of them remembers something distinctive about this Brent guy." Venom drips from Emmett's voice when he says the perpetrator's name. "It doesn't appear that anything was stolen from the apartment, but we'll have you confirm that when we can get you back home."

"Hopefully that'll be today." Elli's voice wavers at the end of her sentence, and I know she's trying to keep it together in front of the detectives.

"If you guys are finished, maybe we can give her a break for now," I say.

I know she probably needs a good cry and doesn't want any of us in here for it. She's strong but she does break occasionally, and when she does there are no witnesses. I learned that early on in our relationship during one finals week. She'd failed one of her exams and then holed up in our apartment for a week, not answering anyone's phone calls or coming out of her room except for when she had to eat or use the bathroom.

"Yeah, we can work on these leads and get back to you later when you've rested. We're here if you need anything. Please don't hesitate to call either of us." Officer Tropp's tone is gentle and steady as she hands Elli her business card.

I can tell she's really good at putting people at ease, which must come in handy in this field of work.

"Raven." He gives me a single nod as he follows his partner out of the room.

"What was that?" Elli looks over at me, eyelashes batting a mile a minute, even though her eyes are still swollen.

If anything can break her out of her silent and brooding spell, it's her curiosity with me and the men I involve myself with.

"Nothing," I say.

"Bullshit. How do you know him?"

I shrug. "Is this really important right now, E?"

"You bet your ass it is. I need something to take my mind off of this shit. Spill."

How am I going to say no to her, while she's lying in a hospital bed, body swollen and black and blue?

"All right, all right," I say, relenting.

"Yessss. I can't wait." Elli is almost giddy, and I'm glad I can provide a little lightness to one of the worst days of her life with my questionable decisions.

Twenty minutes later the beans are spilled and she's staring at me, mouth agape.

"Rave, what in the hell? You don't do this kind of thing."

"I know." I didn't tell her about the creep in the bar; I figure we should save that for when we're not sitting in a hospital room just hours after she was attacked.

"I mean, he's hot. He's really hot."

"I know."

"Like really hot. Did you know he was a cop?"

I consider the question for a second, nervous to tell her the truth.

How am I supposed to tell her I had no idea what he did for work, or that he walked me home because a creep—who sounds like the guy who attacked her—was watching me?

Eight

Emmett

"Nope. I mean I knew there was a chance. The haircut gave him away, plus he's clean shaven and he's definitely in shape."

I stand outside of Miss James' room listening to Raven tell her friend about me. I didn't mean to eavesdrop, but I caught the last snippet of the story and couldn't stop listening.

"And you were planning on never seeing him again, am I right?" Elli asks.

I hear a muffled noise that sounds like a yes.

"And now he shows up here to investigate my *incident*, how convenient!" Elli says, and I can hear the sarcasm loud and clear. "And now you have to see him, so you can't run away. I love it!"

More grumbling from Raven.

"Well, how was it?"

"How was what?" Raven asks.

"You know exactly what, Raven Elyse."

Raven Elyse Jackson. Nice.

"I'm not going to talk about it with you right now, Elli. Come on."

"Yes, you are. You haven't gotten laid in how long? Six months? You are going to tell me. I'm playing the injured victim card this one time and this time only. And this is like, divine intervention or some shit. Spill it, Rave."

"I swear to God, E. Why are you like this?" I hear her chuckle at the end and imagine her grinning. "It was…much needed."

"Nope, I need more than that."

"It was great, okay? Fantastic. Best sex of my life. I came three times. You happy?"

"Very. You better hit that again."

"Elliott! You're relentless. I don't double-dip, you know that. And he's working your case, so that would be some sort of conflict of interest or something. Definitely weird. He's nice, he's cute, but I don't know anything about him and I'm not getting into a relationship, so what's the point? It was a good night. It's over and done with now."

"You've got to let it go. Landry was five years ago, babe. I know it still hurts, but you can't shut everyone out for the rest of your life and live alone above your bookstore forever. You're like a cat lady, but with books."

I hold in a chuckle and imagine the eye-roll Raven is giving her.

"I'm not doing this right now. I love you, I know you mean well, but this isn't the time or the place for that conversation. I need to go out and call Missy and Jason to check on the shop. You okay if I head out for a few? I'll be back, and I'll try to sneak a burger in for you," Raven says.

"Yes, finally. Go. I need a few minutes to myself, anyway. Love you. Extra pickles."

I start walking away from the door when I hear Raven rise from the chair she's been perched in all morning. I was coming back to ask if Elliott would be willing to meet with a sketch artist, but I'll come back in a few hours. It sounds like she needs her space right now, and I can respect that.

I'm waiting for the elevator when I feel Raven come up behind me. I'm holding my breath but I'm not sure why.

The warning Monica got about the ferocious best friend now makes sense.

"You're still here?" She sounds annoyed, but there's a hint of sadness in her words.

I know it's been a rough morning for her.

"Yeah, I'm heading back to the station now to start up some paperwork, but I'll be back later to talk to Miss James some more. Is she holding up okay?"

"Nope. I mean, I know she looks strong and pretty normal considering what just happened to her, but I can tell she's a few minutes away from a breakdown, so I'm letting her have her peace for a bit. She doesn't like to cry in front of anyone."

"You sound like you really understand her. It's good that she has you."

She wraps her arms around herself, fists grabbing handfuls of her hoodie. I can see the worry on her face, so different from the last time I saw her, wrapped in a towel this morning.

"Yeah, we've been best friends for over six years. Met in college. She was pre-law and I was getting my undergrad in psychology. We're night and day but we work."

"I can tell," I say.

The elevator doors open and we step inside, both reaching for the ground floor button. I swear I feel a zing when our hands touch.

How cliché.

"You heading back to your apartment?" I ask her.

She throws me a dirty look. "You mean my store? No, not until later tonight when I can get her settled. And no, you're not invited."

"Ouch. I'm still on duty, you know, wasn't looking for an invite. I've got a pretty big case to work on here." I see the hurt in her eyes and realize how clipped my tone sounded. I feel like an ass but it kind of serves her right. Everything I say isn't a come-on. But then again, given last night she probably isn't sure what's a come-on and what's not. I need to work on my delivery.

"Oh, right. I'm sorry. I can be a bitch. It's a defense mechanism. I won't bore you with the psychology of it. Just know it's not your fault. Not always, anyway."

"Yeah, I read that in a note I found this morning after you bailed." I nudge her shoulder with mine to let her know I'm playing as the doors open and we head into the lobby.

As the physical distance grows between us I get a whiff of her perfume and for a second, I recall how she looked last night underneath me.

"Right, so yeah, I guess I'll see you around." She snaps me out of my daydream. "Let me know if you have any leads, or if you need me to identify him. I think it's the guy from the bar last night. It has to be."

"I'm thinking the same, but we can't be sure so I'm going to explore all the options first. I'll let you know if we need your assistance, though. Thank you."

I watch her walk away, hips swaying naturally as she walks.

I feel a heaviness in my chest thinking about what she went through, finding her friend the way she did this morning. These women are tough, no doubt about that.

I just hope I can do them justice and put this fucker behind bars.

Nine

Raven

I climb into my car and lean my head back against the headrest. It's not even lunch yet and I feel like I've been up for forty-eight hours. I'm sure the late night with Emmett didn't help matters.

I cannot believe the events that have transpired in the last twelve hours.

Last night was amazing. This morning has been hell.

They ran test after test and Elli didn't want me to leave her side during any of it, not that I would have. Then lo and behold, Emmett Mystery-Man Fisher shows up out of the blue. Of all the cops. Of all the detectives.

I think back on the night before and try to remember every detail about the man at the end of the bar who gave off the creepiest vibes I've ever felt. He was wearing a navy jacket, I think. Maybe black. His hair was shaggy and dirty blond. He looked a little unkempt. I wish I could remember more, but all I can recall are the vivid feelings of dread and disappointment that radiated off of him when we walked past him.

He was definitely pissed I was leaving with Emmett.

What if that made him so upset, that he then took that anger out on someone else?

Elliott being the random victim in the wrong place at the wrong time. I should have stayed longer. She always goes out with her girlfriends from work once a month, but they usually stay uptown. I don't think they've ever ventured to the bars downtown. Elli usually goes to the high-class, twenty-dollar martini places close to her condo. I would have never have guessed that she would have gone to the bar by me. Logically, I know it's not my fault, but the guilt is still nagging me.

I pull my cell phone out and check my texts and calls, all Missy and Jason checking on Elli and letting me know everything is fine at the shop. I call Jason and he answers on the first ring, saying he's made about ten sales and Lacey didn't show for her shift. Typical Saturday at *Poe's*.

Yes, Poe's. Edgar Allen Poe. My name is Raven. I had to do it.

Lacey. Ugh.

I'm going to have to bite the bullet and fire her, and I really don't want to deal with that hot mess. She's a college student that stumbled into the store a few months ago, raving about its quirkiness and how it was the perfect place for her. She was so in love with the atmosphere that when she asked if we had any staff openings I couldn't refuse her. Her enthusiasm was contagious, and it made me feel like I'd finally accomplished what I had set out to do—make Poe's one of a kind, and a place that called to every bookworm's heart.

Unfortunately, that enthusiasm was short-lived when she realized she'd have to do actual work during her hours in the shop. Binding and repairing old books, serving refreshments when the occasional patron wanted a coffee, ringing people up, taking inventory. None of that sparked joy for her and now she's flaky at best, coming in for her shifts whenever she feels like it. I should call her now and get it over with.

She answers just before her voicemail picks up. "Raven! Oh my god, hey!"

"Hi, Lacey. What's going on?"

"Oh, nothing. I'm in Sedona. It's amazing!"

"Sedona, Arizona?" I ask her.

"Yes! Isn't that awesome? A friend had last-minute tickets to a festival out here and I tagged along. You should see this place, Raven! The atmosphere!"

I roll my eyes and take a breath. "Lacey, you know you were supposed to work today, right? And the rest of the week?"

"Oh, right. No, I hadn't thought that far ahead. Sorry, you know how I get swept away…"

"Mm hmm, well, this is the fourth time this month that you haven't shown for your shift, and I could've really used the help today. I don't think this is working out, unfortunately. When you get back into town you can pick up your things and your last check. I hope you have a great trip."

"Oh, all right, I understand," she says, and I'm surprised to hear actual disappointment in her voice. "Well, I'll see you next week then. Thank you for understanding."

I end the call and shake my head. If firing you is *understanding,* so be it.

I don't want to go anywhere. In fact, I'd love to take a nap right here in my car, but I promised Elli that I wouldn't be gone long and would get her a burger so I better get a move on. It's a little before eleven but I know she's hungry.

On the way over to the closest burger joint I call one of my psychology friends who specializes in rape victims and their trauma. She does great work with rebuilding their sense of self-worth and confidence. As much as I want to help Elli myself, I know it's a conflict of interest and I'm too close to the situation to see it unbiased. She'll be in the best hands with my friend.

She agrees to come by the hospital later this afternoon. I'm still hoping Elli can go home today, but that will depend on the blood test results that have yet to come back.

I get our burgers and head back to the hospital, sucking down my huge coke on the way to replenish my caffeine levels. I'm not a huge coffee drinker even though I meet Elli at Missy's every Saturday morning. I'd rather have the sugary artificial stuff any day of the week.

Pulling into a spot farther away from the main entrance, I gather my thoughts before going up to Elli's room. I need to put my happy face on. I'm sure Emmett and Detective Tropp are doing their best to catch this guy, and one of the cops that were staying with Elli earlier said that rapists almost never repeat victims when they're random like this. I don't think he'll come back to hurt her again, but I'll feel a lot better when he's off the streets and paying for what he did.

Ten

Emmett

"The lab tech just called, she was definitely drugged. A mixture of a few things, including Rohypnol. That explains why she doesn't remember anything after the elevator. The only broken bones are two ribs on her left side, everything else is just bruised up pretty bad, and the cut above her eye is where most of the blood came from," Monica says.

She's scanning the rest of the reports from the responding officers that we collected earlier. I get a sinking feeling in my chest with the news, but that's quickly replaced with anger.

"It's probably a good thing that she doesn't remember, as awful as it is to say that," she adds. "Maybe that'll help with some of the trauma and the nightmares that are sure to come. She must have put up a hell of a fight, even after being drugged. That apartment was destroyed. Some of the blood on the carpet doesn't belong to her, like we thought. They're running the DNA, but it'll take a few days to get it back."

I nod, hating the way the system works but understanding that our hands are tied. "Have you been able to get in touch with the other two friends of hers from last night?"

"Yep, I spoke with all of them. Beth said that Elliott was talking with a man when she and Lauren left, but neither of them got a solid look at him. Lauren did say that she thought he looked disheveled, and not like someone that Miss James would normally give the time of day to, which corresponds with what River told us."

When we had first gotten back to the station after leaving the hospital, River was there waiting for us, extremely distraught. It took a lot to get her calmed down enough to get a good statement from her. She blamed herself for leaving with the guy she met up with and not staying with Elliott.

After we settled her down enough to talk, she told us that Elli wasn't very into the man, but he wouldn't take no for an answer and she eventually gave in and let him dance with them. River said she thought he was strange, but she wasn't uneasy around him. He just seemed to be trying too hard and got very attached very fast.

"I'm going to head back over to the bar and see if there are security cameras that caught him," I say to Monica. Maybe we'll get lucky and he'll have paid his tab with a card last night. I'll meet you at the hospital in an hour with the sketch artist."

"Sounds good, Fisher."

It takes me a good ten minutes to get to the bar, and when I do they've just opened for the day. The bartender from last night happens to be working the day-shift today and he remembers me. I ask him about the guy at the end of the bar and he says that he's not a regular and he doesn't recall ever seeing him before. I ask if he could check the receipts from last night to see if Brent paid with a card and he goes in the back.

While he's gone, my eyes wander over to the stools that Raven and I had sat in. It could've been her lying in that hospital bed this morning, which makes me feel sick to my stomach. I don't normally get attached like this, and never after one day.

She's something else, though. Beautiful, with her long dark hair and green eyes. Tall and lithe, her body fit perfectly with mine last night. She's obviously smart. I saw her diploma hanging on the wall in her apartment this morning—a Master's Degree in Clinical Psychology from UNC Chapel Hill, where she and Elliott met.

She seems like an amazing friend to Elliott, extremely selfless and giving. But then there's this side of her that is so closed off and hard.

I think back to what they were talking about this morning in the room.

"Landry was five years ago…"

Who the hell is Landry? And why do I want to punch him?

That's got to be why she's so "bitchy" as she says, although I find it adorable—but I wouldn't tell her that. She's a puzzle that I want to figure out. But first I've got to find the guy who did this.

The bartender comes back and has a single receipt with him, which is a good sign. "All I can find is this one receipt in that timeframe, someone named B. Smallwood. Might be him."

I thank him and take a copy of the receipt for evidence. It's not much to go on, and I'm not even sure his real name is Brent Smallwood, but it's a start.

Wrenn Montgomery

Eleven

Raven

I've never been this level of exhausted. I stayed with Elli until they released her, and then I took her back to her penthouse to get her situated and make sure she had all of her meds and anything else she might need.

I finally left after begging her for hours to stay with me until they catch the guy who did this. She refused, of course. But she did hire a security company to stay with her twenty-four/seven—probably more for my comfort than hers. She even made them all come up and introduce themselves to me, and she gave Albert and the night doorman a bonus for the "trouble" she'd put them through.

She seems to be dealing with this like a champ, but I'm waiting for the other shoe to drop. If/when it does, I'll be there for her.

It's late, after nine, and I realize I haven't had any dinner. I mentally run through the groceries in my fridge and decide I'll have bacon again.

That's a balanced meal, right?

I almost decide against it because it reminds me of last night with Emmett, and then quickly determine that's *exactly* why I'm going to fix myself an entire pound anyway.

I will not let some man taint bacon for me.

I unlock the shop and breathe in the smell. The smell that Emmett blamed that first kiss on. The fact that he blamed it on old books made me want him even more. I wonder if he's a bookworm like me, or if he just gets off on the sexy librarian type.

It doesn't matter, Raven. You're not going to see him again other than professionally.

As I step in and close the door behind me, I feel something crinkle under my feet and realize I'm stepping on an envelope that had been jammed underneath the door. My name is scrawled across the top and for a second my heart speeds up, foolishly hoping it's from Emmett. The letters are small and slanted, not like his large block numbers from earlier. I never did give him my number, but I'm sure he could have gotten it from the police reports.

I tear open the envelope and flip the paper over, only to drop it a second later.

The text is typed in big and bold black capitals. There's no signature, no return address, only one sentence.

I scramble over to the desk where I left the note that I wrote for Emmett earlier, where his number is scrawled across the bottom. Hands trembling, I call him and pray to God he answers.

"Detective Fisher," he says.

"Emmett?"

"Raven?"

"Are you busy?" I ask him.

"I just got off, headed home. You all right?"

"No, I'm not. Can you come by here? There was a letter under my door. I think you need to see it." My voice is shaking, and I'm sure it's obvious how freaked out I am. I'm trying to hold it together but failing.

"Yes, I'm coming right now. I'll be there in ten. Tell me what it says, gorgeous."

I take a deep breath and blow it out before answering him, trying to steady my voice. "It says, 'It was supposed to be you, Bitch.'"

Wrenn Montgomery

Twelve

Emmett

Fuck. Fuck, fuck, fuck.

I want to have Raven stay on the phone with me until I get there, but I need to call this in so we can log the letter and envelope as evidence. "I'm on the way, lock the door. Get that pistol out and sit in the corner with your back against the wall. If you hear anything or you get scared at all, call nine-one-one and get the hell out of there."

"How did you know about the pistol?"

"Raven, I'm a cop. I can spot a concealed weapon a mile away." I don't tell her that watching her grip that pistol hidden in her purse the night before turned me on more than the damn bookstore did. "Just get it out. I'll be there as soon as I can. Don't panic, okay?" But I know she's already panicking.

We hang up and I immediately call the station. Of course it's Alex who answers.

Fuck me.

"Alex." I don't call him Detective Sams out of spite. "I'm en route to Raven Jackson's house. I need an evidence tech sent out there ASAP." I rattle off the address to him, keeping it short and sweet, not giving him any details. He can read the reports like everyone else.

I make it to Raven's bookstore in seven minutes, where I park out front then knock on the door. The pull-down blinds are closed and I can't see inside, but I can hear her walking across the wooden floors.

When the door swings open, I can tell she's trying to remain calm, but she looks like she's ten seconds away from losing it. Her eyes are wild as she looks past me into the street.

I want to pull her in my arms and keep her safe, but right now I'm an officer responding to a call and I need to be professional. At least until the evidence is logged and we're alone again.

"I didn't think I'd ever see you back here." She chuckles after she says it, like she's nervous and trying to divert.

I can appreciate that.

"And why not?" I play the game to keep her calm.

"I don't do repeats. And I was rude to you this morning."

"Well, apparently rude kinda does it for me. Show me the note."

So much for being professional.

She rolls her eyes and locks the door behind us.

I let her know that the evidence tech should be here any minute so she's not alarmed when they knock. Then, I grab a glove out of my back pocket and head over to where the letter is sitting on her desk.

She stands beside me wringing her hands, avoiding looking at it with me.

The note has classic stalker written all over it. No identifying handwriting, aside from her name on the envelope which wasn't licked closed. Basic paper. The only thing strange is that they capitalized "Bitch" like it was a name.

Raven is worrying her lip with her teeth, looking around her shop nervously, like she's scared someone might jump out. I start doing a sweep of the rooms to ease her mind and mine. The rows and rows of books of every color and kind are a marvel to look at and I wish I had extra time to browse like I was a customer.

There's a corner in the back with cozy-looking and mismatched furniture in every shade. Quite a contrast to her life upstairs. I wonder if she lives in color for everyone else but survives in neutral tones when she's alone.

I finish sweeping the main room, the attached storage room, and the large closet where she repairs books. Nothing appears to be disturbed.

"He was stalking me," she says. "He was there because I was, and when I left with you he took it out on Elli."

I sigh because I know she could be right, but I don't know what to say to make it better. "Have you ever had a stalker or received any threatening messages like this before?"

"No. Never."

"Do you know anyone who might want to hurt you?"

"Not that I know of…"

"Any exes who might do something like this?" I ask.

"I…no." Her answer is quick and short.

I can't help but think there may be more to it, however, it's not up to me to pry. Maybe she'll tell Monica more. I make a mental note to have Tropp come by to check on her tomorrow and see if she can get any more information out of her.

A knock at the door tells me that the evidence tech is here, and Raven says she's going to go upstairs and run a bath.

"You're welcome to stay." She trails off as she says it like it pains her to do so, and I'm sure it does.

Probably half from her "no repeats" rule and half from her being too scared to stay here alone but not wanting to admit it.

I just nod, not making any jokes. I know this is hard for her.

Twenty minutes later the letter is on its way to the station and I've finished my report of today's events. I make sure the shop is locked up before heading upstairs to check on her.

The bathroom door is cracked open and steam is rolling out. I hear gentle splashes as she moves around in there. The scent of candles burning fills the air, and there's a bottle of wine open on the countertop in the kitchenette. I know this isn't a romantic ruse. This must be how she unwinds after a stressful day, and I don't want to disturb her.

While I was downstairs I snagged a book from one of the loaner shelves. It's worn, like it's been read more than a few times. I wonder if it's one of her favorites.

Settling into her couch, I start reading. It's an author I've never heard of, but I like the tempo and rhythm of the words. It's a romance, but it's written in a masculine tone. It's not long before I'm lost in it, the chapters flying by.

Sometime later I feel someone staring at me and glance over. Raven is lying on her bed, completely naked.

My cock jumps to attention, but I want to make sure before I make any moves from where I'm sitting. "Do you usually sleep naked?"

"Never."

"Is this an invitation?"

She just stares at me and tilts her head to the side. "If you want to take it."

I'm over there in less than two seconds saying, "Are you sure that you're up to this? It's been a rough—"

"Stop talking."

So I do, and for the next two hours her body is mine and I make damn sure that's all she's thinking about.

Thirteen

Raven

Sundays are my days to sleep in. I don't have to open the shop until noon, so I usually lie in bed until at least ten. I'm not a morning person, therefore I consider it my reward for getting up all week and being an adult. And after the last few days I've had, I need it now more than ever.

The only problem with that is there's an extremely large, extremely attractive, extremely dangerous man curled around me right now and I can't fall back asleep. And by dangerous, I don't mean the scared-for-my-safety kind. He's a cop, for God's sake. I don't think I could be in better hands as far as that's concerned.

However, my heart is an entirely different story. This is why I only do one-night stands. Otherwise, feelings get involved, people get attached. It never ends well. Not that I'm attached to him, I just feel like I *could* see how someone—not me, but *someone*—could possibly get attached to him.

I don't know his story. I don't know where he was born, where he lives, why he became a cop, what the bullet-shaped scar on his side is from.

I don't know anything about him.

But if he's going to keep sharing my bed, it's time to learn those things. The problem is I know he'll have questions of his own and I don't know if I'm ready to answer them.

Last night when I came out of the shower, he was reading and so immersed in the book that he didn't notice me for twenty minutes. The fact that he had chosen one of my favorites—without knowing—and seemed to be appreciating it as much as I do, really did something for me.

I took the opportunity to stare at him and take in all of his features. His dark hair, so short. The beginning of a tattoo peeking out under his short sleeve that I hadn't noticed the night before. I see now that it wraps around his bicep and up onto his shoulder. It's a mix of patriotic symbols and words, and I don't recognize the language.

But the fact that he was comfortable just sitting on my couch and reading—*hello, sexiest quality a man can have*—instead of interrupting my bath, tells me he understands me more than I'd like.

He stirs beside me and pulls me closer to him. Even though I don't know anything about him, it feels like our bodies know each other. Our minds just aren't on the same page yet.

His eyes slowly open and he immediately turns his head to me.

"Morning, sunshine," I chirp to him.

"What time is it?" His voice comes out as a deep rumble.

"A little after eight. Do you have to work today?"

"No, it's my day off, but I do need to go in for a bit and see if anything has come of the letter." He winces as he says the last word, like he didn't mean to bring it up and ruin the moment.

"It's fine," I reassure him. "I'm okay. I mean I was scared for sure. I'm still a little uneasy but I'm all right. I'm hoping that whoever left the letter doesn't know I live here and just expected me to find it this morning when I came into the shop."

"I'm going to have an officer patrol the area outside the shop when I'm not here, just until we can figure out what we're dealing with and catch whoever's behind this."

I like how he says "when I'm not here" like he plans on being here a lot.

"Any ideas?" I ask him.

"I'm honestly not sure. At this point it could be anyone. We need to keep our options open." He wraps his arm tighter around my back and starts to rub small circles there.

I roll away from him to put a little distance between us, feeling oddly exposed by the sweet gesture.

"Who is Landry, Raven?"

My blood runs cold and goosebumps break out across my skin. "Where did you hear that name?"

"I overheard the end of your conversation with Elli yesterday."

"You were eavesdropping?" I ask him.

"I didn't mean to. I was coming back to ask her something and heard my name, followed by his. Is he the reason you're so closed off?"

I shrug, not really wanting to go there. I'm pissed that he was eavesdropping, accidentally or not. "Probably so."

"Can you tell me about him? I know it's none of my business and you don't have to. But I—"

"People only want to know what they're up against so they can make a battle plan," I say.

"That's true. Do you want me to win this battle, Raven?"

In the two seconds it takes for his question to settle over me, I realize I do.

Wrenn Montgomery

Fourteen

Emmett

Raven takes a deep breath and I brace myself. Whatever she's about to say is going to be monumental, and she seems nervous.

"Landry and I dated all through college. At first, our relationship was your normal college fling. I didn't want anything serious, he wanted a fuck buddy, it worked out. He was thoughtful and generous. He'd remember when my tests were and send me good luck flowers. He'd take me on super romantic dates and woo me relentlessly. Eventually he fell for me and wanted more. I gave in, and began to feel the same way toward him as the relationship progressed. Landry came from a wealthy family. His dad was a lawyer and his mom was the perfect Stepford wife. His parents even offered to pay for my college because they thought we'd be getting married."

She looks up at the ceiling, avoiding looking at me like she's ashamed of how she felt about him.

"I did come to love him, though now I know it wasn't love. It was some version of it that felt like love, but you don't treat people you love the way he treated me. I shouldn't have accepted their offer to pay my tuition, but I almost felt like it was my payment for having to deal with their son and keep him on the right path, and I think his parents thought that, too.

That doesn't make it right, but it's the truth. We moved in together our sophomore year. That's when things started getting worse. He always had a temper. When he drank too much, which happened often, he'd get mad at the way the towels were folded, or something would stop working in the apartment and he'd completely overreact. He'd throw things and yell. It would take a while to calm him down but he would eventually pass out. I thought that it was just the spoiled brat coming out in him from the way he was raised. But then it began to escalate.

He never hit me, but he would grab my wrists, push me away from him, throw things at me instead of the wall. He was emotionally abusive, called me every name in the book, but 'bitch' was his favorite. I don't know why I didn't leave. I felt responsible for him, like I could fix him."

She rolls her eyes here, like it's hard for her to admit that she felt this way. She seems like she doesn't want to seem vulnerable, but here she is spilling her guts to me anyway.

"He started staying out late, being gone for hours past when he said he'd be home. He'd tell me that he had work trips he had to go on, and I later found out that he had been fired months before then. I assumed he was cheating on me. I thought if I could catch him, I'd have solid proof and it would make it easier to leave him. I know that sounds crazy now, looking back, but I felt like he was a good guy that was going through a hard time. Elli and I were getting close at this point, and she was always on his case. He hated her and didn't want me around her, but I also think he respected her. One night, Elli talked me into following him when he told me he was going to a work dinner in the town next to ours. We looked like idiots wearing all black and tailing him in Elli's old Toyota Camry with a bumper half hanging off."

A faint smile appears on her lips as she remembers before she continues.

"When we pulled up to the hotel I was convinced he was meeting a girl there. Elli went inside to watch him while he checked in, to see if she could hear which room he was staying in. She did, and then she booked the room right beside his. We waited until he left for the 'work meeting' before we went up to our room so he wouldn't see us. The rooms connected with a door, which was locked, of course, but we could hear pretty well through it. The plan was that we'd wait until we knew he was in there with the girl, and then we'd knock on his door and I'd confront him. Only, he didn't bring a girl back. He brought several men back to the room. We were confused. Elli was convinced he was gay and had some weird orgy going on."

She rolls her eyes again before continuing. "But through the door we could hear them outlining their plan. Landry was at the head of it all. From what we could tell, they were importing illegal drugs and selling them to the students at the college. We stood there, mouths agape, and Elli started recording him on her phone. They were planning on killing another big drug dealer in the area and taking over his territory. Apparently business wasn't going well, and they needed to start selling to the locals instead of just the college crowd to pay back some debt they owed to their dealer. Landry was planning the murder and telling the others where the victim was going to be that night. We stopped listening because we were terrified, and we snuck out of the hotel and booked it back to my apartment. Once we were there, we called the police and played the recording for the officer who came out. They sent units out, but it was too late. The other guy had been killed and Landry was driving the car in the drive-by.

Twenty cops swarmed the house and found cocaine and heroin in the walls behind our bed. I was so clueless. I was in shock. They brought me in for questioning and I told them everything I knew. Landry was caught and brought in the same night. I was still there when they brought him in, and the look on his face when he saw me and realized I was the reason he had gotten caught is something I'll never forget. He's been in jail for the last five years, and I was told he'd face at least twenty before being eligible for parole. He was charged with second-degree murder and drug distribution. His parents were devastated. It was a hard time in my life, but it's in the past."

She lies back on the pillow and stares up at the ceiling, and I do the same so I can process everything she just said.

I wrap my arm around her and pull her closer to me. I know we're not dating. I don't know what this is, but it's more than just fucking, and I feel the need to let her know I'm not going anywhere, regardless of her past.

Fifteen

Raven

I feel better after spilling my guts to Emmett. Until he leaves.

He said he was going into the station to work, and I know he has to, but I'm hoping that his departure didn't have anything to do with him wanting to distance himself from me after what I told him.

I did what I had to do. I stayed with Landry like a fucking idiot when I should have left at the first red flag. But when you're twenty, hearing someone tell you they'll pay your college tuition for dating their wayward son and keeping him on track sounds like a hell of a deal. And it was so good in the beginning. I really did think he loved me, and vice versa.

Now, I know that our entire relationship was a front. He needed to look like he had his head on straight for me, and for his parents who were funding his lifestyle. The "job" he had gotten fired from without me knowing was an internship at the financial firm he was set to be hired at upon graduation.

What a joke.

The whole thing is a joke, but it's a joke that left me broken, bruised, and not trusting a damn soul.

I call Elli to check on her; she says she's sore and the swelling is a little worse today, but that she feels better than she did yesterday.

I don't tell her about the letter. I will when we know something for sure. There's no point in worrying her right now. I promise her I'll come over later with her favorite Mexican takeout when the shop closes and we hang up.

I still have about an hour until the shop opens, so I run down to Missy and Jason's and order an iced coffee. Even though it's February, it's the only kind of coffee I can tolerate.

I sit at a table in the corner so the wall is behind me. I try not to constantly look over my shoulder like a paranoid mess, but it's hard.

My mind drifts back to Emmett and our conversation from earlier. I revealed something huge about my past but I still don't know anything about him or where he came from. The next time I see him I'm going to ask him some questions, even the playing field a little. I know he doesn't *owe* me anything, but it would be nice to feel like I didn't just bare my soul to someone I barely know.

I finish drinking my iced coffee and head back to start opening the shop.

There's already a small line waiting for me when I get there. Sundays are the busiest days for some reason—usually double the sales—and it's nice having the shop so full. It seems like everyone just wants to hang out in the lounge on their lazy day and read a good book. It's the best time for people watching at Poe's.

I unlock and let the early bird patrons in five minutes before opening time and take my perch behind the desk, in front of the hidden staircase that leads to my apartment.

My cell phone rings and I answer it while starting up the operating system I use for sales and book lending. I don't recognize the number but it's a local area code. "Hello?"

"Raven? It's Emmett. This is my office number. Save it in case you ever need me and can't get me on my cell."

In case I ever need him.

Why is part of me wishing he wasn't referring to the case? What the hell is wrong with me?

"All right," I say. "Did you need something?"

"I just wanted to let you know that we weren't able to get any DNA from the letter, and the paper is a standard kind from any office supply store."

"I figured as much. So that's a dead-end?"

"Basically. We're still working on a few things. I'll keep you as updated as I can," he tells me.

"I know you can't tell me everything, but I really appreciate it."

"Can I see you tonight?"

My heart skips a beat. When he left earlier we didn't say that we'd see each other later, we just sort of left it open. I was worried I'd scared him off with my story.

"Three nights in a row, Emmett?" I ask with a little snark.

"Yeah, three nights in a row. What time do you want me to come over?" His all-business tone does something to me.

"I told Elli I'd bring her some dinner later. I'll probably hang out with her for a while, so maybe nine?" I try not to sound as excited as I feel.

Honestly, thinking about staying the night alone gives me a little anxiety knowing someone knows where my apartment is, or at least where the store is, and I haven't spent a full night alone since the night Elli was attacked.

"See you then, gorgeous."

I sigh and end the call, then catch Ms. Isley—one of my regulars—grinning at me from an old worn arm chair across the room. She winks, and I blush before turning to help the customer who's approached the desk with a pile of new releases.

The day passes quickly and when it's ten past five the last patron leaves and I lock up before heading to Elli's. I call in our order at *El Cantino's* and think of Elli the entire ride there and then to her apartment.

We have to get to the bottom of this, for each of our sakes.

Sixteen

Emmett

I throw my reading glasses onto my desk and rub my eyes. I've been pouring over case notes for the last few hours, trying to find a connection or a lead.

If it weren't for the note sent to Raven's shop, we wouldn't even know she was a target. They wanted the note to point us toward her and her circle, but why? Raven seems to think she has no enemies, no one that would want to see her or her friends hurt. There's an ex in prison, who is our number one suspect due to the circumstances. Paying him a visit is at the top of my list. But what could we be missing here?

"You need a coffee?" Monica lingers at my door, looking every bit as tired as I am.

"Yeah, thanks."

She nods but doesn't leave right away. "Can I talk to you for a second?"

"Sure, what's up?" I shuffle the papers to the side so I can focus on whatever she needs to say. From what I can tell so far, she's not a person of many words, so this must be important.

"Your head's in your ass," she says bluntly.

I stare at her, not knowing what to say.

"You have a thing for the friend," she clarifies.

"I mean, I went home with her the night of—"

"I know that. That's not what I'm asking."

I weigh my options. I like Monica, but we've only been partners for a few days. I'm not sure how much I can trust her yet. If she thinks I'm too close to Raven, she can tell the captain to pull me off the case. "Yeah, I've got a thing for her. But it's not affecting my—"

"Again, not what I asked. I think it's going to make you work harder on this case. I just want to make sure you're not going to lose your head over it, understand?"

I nod, relieved we're on the same page. "I'm good."

"Great. I'll grab that coffee."

I think I see a hint of a smile as she walks out of my office, and I let out a breath I didn't know I was holding.

I don't know what I'm doing with Raven. It's not surprising that I feel this need to keep her safe. I'm a protector by birth. I'm the oldest of three siblings and I spent my childhood protecting them. I joined the Marines the day after my high school graduation with all intent to be a lifer.

When I got injured last year, I was medically retired but I knew I wouldn't be happy with a normal civilian job. So, I became a cop. I have always protected those around me. But I have never felt this immediate need to protect a grown woman the way I do now.

Raven is extremely independent. She turns me away every chance she gets. But I know deep down, under all those trust issues and in that bruised heart, she wants someone that will be there for her when she wants them to be.

There's nothing wrong with depending only on yourself, but sometimes that gets old and you need another shoulder to lean on.

I want to be that for her, if only she'll let me.

A quick look in the prisoner tracking database tells me Landry is in a prison not too far from here, so I decide to head down there and check things out.

It's a thirty-minute drive, and I blast music the entire way to keep my thoughts off of Raven. It works, but barely.

Pulling up to the prison, an uneasy feeling settles in my gut. The crimes the people in this facility have committed. The people they've hurt. I won't allow Raven to become one of them.

I clip my badge onto my belt and head in, steeling my face and emotions into the detective I am, not some lovesick boyfriend paying a visit to an ex.

The man behind the front desk looks like he could be my grandfather, surely past retirement age.

His dark-rimmed coke bottle glasses sit perched on the end of his nose, and he looks up at me as I walk in, noting my badge first. "Detective, what can I do for you?"

"Emmett Fisher. I was hoping I could question one of your prisoners, Landry Davis."

He starts typing on his computer, hunting and pecking away. "I'm sorry, sir, that's not possible."

"I'm sorry?"

"Landry Davis was killed three weeks ago in a fight that broke out in the yard. The investigation is still underway, but they're thinking it was gang related, possibly in relation to his charges."

Fuck.

I don't know if this will hurt Raven or bring her peace, but at least we know he can't be behind the attacks.

"I'm sorry to hear that," I offer.

"Would you like the investigator on the case to give you a call?"

I say yes, thank him, and give him my contact info, then I'm back on the road.

How the hell do I tell Raven this news?
And how is she going to take it?

Wrenn Montgomery

Seventeen

Raven

"Finally!" she says.

"I called you when I was leaving the shop. That was only twenty minutes ago, E."

"I know, but I'm starving. And twenty minutes feels like two hours when you're stuck in this condo all day."

"You should come stay with me." I shuffle into her foyer as she takes some of the bags from me.

"No, Rave. I'm comfortable here. I've got security. Plus, I don't want to bring this to your doorstep if he comes back."

"Yeah…"

"What?" she asks.

"Nothing." I quickly turn my back to her and beeline for her kitchen, stopping at the liquor cabinet.

"You're not telling me something. What is it?" Her voice is closer, coming up behind me. She's not going to let me get away easily.

Finally spotting the tequila, I attempt to dodge again. "It's nothing, just eat your food. You want me to make you a margarita?"

"You know I can't drink with this pain medicine. Your attempts to distract me with alcohol are no good here, babe."

I take a deep breath and spill, filling her in on last night's events.

When I'm finished, I flip the blender on, successfully buying myself some time for her to process before she can speak. I turn slowly to find her peeking over my shoulder.

Her face is a steel vault, just like her emotions. "You mean whoever attacked me, may have actually been after you?"

"It appears that way, Elli. I'm so sorry. I didn't know you'd be going to the bar or I would've stayed. I should have—"

"Stop. Stop right there. I know you. You think this is your fault and it isn't. I would go through that a hundred times so you wouldn't have to go through it instead. Do you hear me? Don't you waste any more energy feeling bad about this. Understood?"

I take another deep breath and nod. I tell her everything. How I met Emmett, why he walked me home. How one thing led to another and he ended up in my bed. How awkward the next morning was. And of course, how that led to the run-in at the hospital.

She takes a second to think, and I can see her head spinning. "Talk about a love story." She starts walking back toward the living room, and I follow her, sitting down at the coffee table to eat.

For some reason, I start cackling and I can't stop. She joins in and soon we're lying on the floor in tears.

"I know, and when he left this morning—"

"I'm sorry, what? When Emmett left *this morning*?" Her voice reaches a new octave at the end of the question and I wince.

Damn it, Raven.

"Uh, yeah. He stayed again last night. After I found the note I was freaked out and he came over. I don't think he wanted me to be there alone."

Nor did I want to be.

"So you, Miss I'm-Tough-as-Shit, just let him stay with you? For the second night in a row?" she asks, seeing right through me, as always.

"Yep."

"Holy shit. I don't even know what to say. You must really like him. What is he like? Does he like you back? Have you seen his apartment? Has he ever been married? What's his story?" She sits up and I follow, digging into our food.

"Elli, we've spent two nights together. I don't know the answers to any of those questions. And this isn't high school, I don't know if he likes me back. He likes the sex and I'm sure he feels obligated to stay with me since he's the one who walked me home from the bar that night."

"No man is going to feel obligated to protect someone after a one-night stand. But you're right, I'm sorry I bombarded you. It's just that it's been five years since I've heard you even mention anyone of the opposite sex other than the guys you banged and ditched."

"Wow, Elli." But I know she's right.

She chuckles and leans back against the couch. "I can't wait to see this unfold."

I roll my eyes and we finish dinner.

I try not to rush but I do, and I know it's because I want to get back home to see Emmett.

But I wouldn't admit that to anyone. Ever.

Wrenn Montgomery

Eighteen

Emmett

I pull up to Poe's at eight forty-five, even though she said nine.

I park out front on the street and notice a black sedan a few spots down. There appears to be someone inside, and my curiosity is spiked.

Who would be casing out a store downtown at this time on a Sunday?

Unless they're waiting for someone…

I get my cell out and call Raven.

She answers on the second ring. "Couldn't wait?"

"I really couldn't, but that's not the only reason I'm calling."

"What's wrong?" She must hear the worry in my voice because her tone goes from flirty to alarmed *that* quick.

"I'm not sure. There's a car sitting a few spots down from your store. I'm going to approach the vehicle. I want you to pull in to the back lot of the store so they don't see you come home, all right? Just to be safe."

"Okay, I'm two blocks away. Stay on the phone with me?"

"Yeah, gorgeous, I'm here." I get out of my SUV and start walking toward the car from behind, staying in their blind spot.

As I get closer I see an older man sitting behind the wheel, ball cap pulled down low over his brow, wearing dark clothing.

I tap on the window and startle him.

He starts the car and tries to put it in drive but he's fumbling.

"Roll down the window," I order.

He shakes his head and gets the car in drive.

I catch a glimpse of a tattoo on his forearm as he turns the wheel and drives off. It's some sort of Celtic knot and I know I've seen it before, but I can't remember where.

"Raven, you still there?"

"Yes, I'm getting ready to pull in now. Are they gone?"

"Yeah, the guy drove away but I got his tags. I'm coming to the front door to wait on you while I call it in. I'll see you in a second."

I wait until I see the lights come on in her shop before I hang up and dial the station.

Guess who answers?

"Miss me that much?" he jokes.

"Alex, I've got some tags, can you pass me to dispatch?"

"Sure thing, but you know you're going to have to speak to me eventually. We work at the same department. We're brothers."

"Maybe we used to be, but that ended when you were balls deep in my girlfriend." I end the call and text Tropp the plate number; she'll get further than I will with Alex.

The door swings open and Raven is there, eyebrows raised to the ceiling.

"Who's balls deep in your girlfriend?" Her tone isn't playful and she's looking at me like she's not sure if she trusts me.

"*Ex*-girlfriend. That was my *ex*-partner, whom I found balls deep in my *then*-girlfriend Friday evening before I went to the bar."

"Oh. So I'm a rebound?" Her voice is lighter now but I can tell there's a lot to her question.

"No, Raven, you're not a rebound. I don't know what this is, but it's already ten times stronger than what I had with Jenna and we're only three days in. I mean, I was upset for sure, but mostly because my partner fucked me over. Someone I was supposed to trust with my life was going home and fucking my girlfriend every night on his dinner break."

"I'm sorry. That's awful."

"It is, but it's over, and it led me here so I'm getting over it pretty quickly."

She looks skeptical but pulls me into the store and locks the door behind us.

"The man in the car...he had a tattoo on his forearm. It looked like a Celtic knot. Do you know anyone with a tattoo like that?" I ask her.

She thinks for a few seconds and says, "No. I don't think so. I'll ask around, though. I'd like to hear more, about your girlfriend, and I guess just about you in general. I feel like I know you, but I don't *know* you."

I figured this would come sooner or later, and I have nothing to hide so I don't mind telling her anything. I'll tell her about Landry afterward. "Okay. Let's talk."

She leads the way to the hidden staircase and up to her home. "Do you drink? I can open a bottle of wine or I have beer in the fridge."

"A beer would be nice, thanks." I head over to the couch and settle in while she grabs the drinks.

As much as I'd like to get her in bed right now, I know she needs this and it's best if we play it safe on the couch.

She comes to sit beside me and tosses her legs over my lap, like we've done this a hundred times. And for some reason, it feels like we have.

"Okay, gorgeous. Ask away."

Wrenn Montgomery

Nineteen

Raven

I feel giddy at the chance to get a glance into Emmett's world, and the fact that he seems so open to whatever I'm going to ask him makes me feel like I can trust him to tell me the truth.

There's comfort in knowing you don't have to pull every bit of information out of a person to get to know them.

I decide to start simple and build my way up. "Where did you grow up?"

"Delaware. A really small town called Millsboro. You?"

"About an hour north of here. Why did you move here?"

"I joined the Marines when I graduated high school, I was injured and medically retired—"

"So that's what the scar is from? Were you shot?"

He chuckles at my interruption. "Yes, and yes. When I got out I didn't want to go back to Delaware. There was nothing there for me. One of my buddies in the Marines is from North Carolina and always talked about how beautiful it was, so I looked for job openings here and went through BLET (Basic Law Enforcement Training) school before getting a job at the department. I moved up to detective pretty quickly because of my military experience, and I really enjoy what I do now."

"What did you do in the Marines?" I ask him.

His eyes darken slightly, and I think he's not going to answer, but he does. "Infantry. I was deployed a few times, nothing major. I miss it a little, and I had a hard time at first because I planned to be a twenty plus career man, but things don't always work out as you plan."

He sounds wistful, so I move on to the next subject before he closes down. "Do you have a family? Where are your parents?"

"My dad is in jail, my mom died when I was young. I have two younger brothers. They both joined the Marines when they were old enough. Emerson is stationed in Jacksonville, another reason I chose North Carolina to move to, and Everette is in California. I fly out to visit him a few times a year."

Of course my mind starts spinning.

Deceased mom, dad in jail, three boys who joined the military instead of sticking around.

I'm sure they had a hard childhood.

"I'm so sorry to hear that, about your mom. And I guess your dad, too. That can't be easy." I don't want to pry and ask what happened to either of them. If he wants to tell me, he will.

"Don't be. I miss my mom but I don't really remember her. She died from breast cancer when I was six. Emerson was four and Everette was two. My dad couldn't handle it, turned to drugs and got too caught up in it. It was just me and the boys. We finally landed in a good foster home right before I turned eighteen. It's the only reason I joined the Marines after high school instead of waiting until Everette was of age. Our foster mom was a saint."

I hear the *was* and I want to ask what happened to her, but he's staring at the wall behind me so I give him a minute to regroup.

"What about you? Any family?" he asks me.

I take a deep breath. *I knew this would come up.* "I never knew my dad. He took off when I was really young. My mom sounds a lot like your dad. She's out of jail right now, but I'm sure she'll be going back soon. I cut off all communication with her a few years back. It was too toxic. No siblings, just me."

I wait as he studies me, unsure of what he's going to say.

He moves his hands from where he was rubbing my legs and grabs my face as he turns to me. Leaning in, I feel his breath on my lips as he hovers there. "Is question time over, gorgeous?"

I nod.

"Good." His lips press softly against mine.

This is different than our other kisses, which have been passionate and rushed.

He slides his lips across mine and I open to let him in. His tongue darts in and I taste the beer he's been sipping on. My legs are still in his lap, but he's turned so that he can lean over me as he pushes me back onto the couch.

I can feel his hardness pressing against my stomach and I reach down to rub him through his pants. His sharp intake of breath emboldens me and I start undoing his belt. He's peppering kisses down my jaw and neck, slow and soft. I sit up so he can slide my shirt over my head and he unhooks my bra in one fluid movement, letting the straps slide down my arms as my breasts spill out.

"You're so fucking beautiful, Raven."

I hate compliments, but coming from him, when he's out of breath and looking like he could eat me up, I take this one and smile back at him.

He kisses down my chest, taking his time with each breast before continuing lower, down my stomach, then he pulls my leggings and panties off when he gets to my waistband.

When I feel his breath against my clit I close my eyes and lose myself in the moment, enjoying every minute of Emmett Fisher and thanking God I changed my mind about going back for seconds.

Twenty

Emmett

I pick Raven up and carry her to bed, her body soft and pliable in my arms after coming again and again on my tongue.

As much as I want to relieve the ache between my legs, I get in the bed behind her and wrap my arms around her.

"What are you doing? Come here. Let me help with that," she says as she wiggles her ass against my groin, not helping matters.

"Shh, you're exhausted. That can wait. Let me hold you." I feel her tense up and I worry she's going to bolt again, but she relaxes in my arms as she turns her head to me, still grinding against me.

"Emmett, I'll decide when I'm exhausted." She gives one last thrust against me and my resolve vanishes.

I grab a condom from her nightstand and jerk my boxers down, rolling the wrapper on as quickly as possible and thrusting into her from behind without warning.

Her sharp intake of breath has me pausing but she immediately picks up the tempo and keeps grinding against me.

I'm not going to last long. Watching her come like that was almost all I could take, and the noises she's making now are about to send me over the edge.

She whispers my name and that does it.

With one final thrust I'm spent, and we lie there for what feels like an hour, basking in the afterglow of what just happened.

"That was…"

"Yeah," I reply.

I was thinking it, too. What we just did wasn't just *fucking*, and that's a first for me.

I've always prided myself on making sure the woman I'm with finishes and is taken care of first, but I've never spent an hour going down on someone just because I wanted to, for the thrill of watching her. Things are different with Raven. I don't want to scare her—hell, I don't want to scare myself—but I could see this, *us*, being a thing. Coming home to her, reading beside her, going to bed with her every night.

She tenses like she can read my mind. "I don't do relationships, Emmett. I know everyone says that and then they cave in the end, but I really can't. I like…this. Whatever it is. And I want it to keep going, if you do. But I don't want to put a label on it and I don't want it to be anything serious."

I smirk, knowing she can't see me. She's already broken one of her rules for me. I've stayed with her the last three nights in a row, every day that I've known her actually. If she needs to not label this for her own peace of mind and so she can try to convince herself this isn't happening, so be it. I'll be here when she changes her mind.

"All right, gorgeous. But if we're doing this, I'm not sleeping with anyone else and I'd like for that to be the case for you also."

"That's not a problem."

"Okay, deal," I say.

"Deal."

My eyes open and it's still dark out. Raven is wrapped around me like a blanket and her breathing is even and slow. She's still asleep.

What woke me?

And then I hear it, her phone vibrating on the counter.

Who would be calling her at three in the morning?

Immediately I think of Elli and I try to rouse her. "Raven, wake up. Your phone is ringing. It might be Elli."

Her eyes fly open and she's across the room in a blur of my white undershirt. "Elli?" Her face morphs from concern to fear, and then anger. She hangs up the phone and slams it down on the counter. "It wasn't Elli." Her voice is monotone.

"Who was it?"

"I don't know, they just started laughing when I answered and said 'See you soon' then hung up." She's scared but she's trying to hide it with anger.

I get up and go to her. "It's all right, Raven. We're going to catch whoever is doing this, and I'm here. I'm not leaving you. Come back to bed while I call dispatch and do a verbal report. Maybe they can trace the call. It's gonna be okay."

I lead her back to bed and as she gets in I see the tears forming. I hate when women cry, but I especially hate when someone I care about cries and I can't fix it.

I make my phone call as quickly as I can—I'm sure raising some red flags as to why I'm with Raven in the middle of the night, but I'll deal with that later.

I need to get back in bed and comfort Raven, because I know she won't ask for help on her own.

Wrenn Montgomery

Twenty-One

Raven

Last night freaked me out pretty bad, and I never thought I'd be so thankful for whatever is going on with me and Emmett.

When I woke up this morning he had already showered and made us breakfast. I secretly loved that he smelled like my shampoo when he kissed me goodbye before he left. Knowing he'll be working on the case all day has me a little nervous. I heard him tell someone at the station that it was escalating when he did his verbal report. First the letter, then someone sitting outside of my apartment yesterday, and lastly, the phone call.

See you soon? Does that mean they're going to attack again, or that it's someone I know and see regularly?

How ironic. The girl who doesn't trust anyone now can't even trust the people she thought she could.

I open the shop and call to check on Elli, also enlightening her on the phone call so she knows to keep her security close.

"Did it sound like anyone you know?" she asks me.

"No, it didn't sound like a familiar voice, but it was only three words and I was half-asleep. And they called from a blocked number, of course."

"Ugh, I'm so over this. They need to catch the guy behind this and end it. I know they're trying their best, but I'm ready to be able to leave my apartment without twelve security guards."

"I know, E. I'm sorry."

"What did I tell you about being sorry for something that is not your fault?" she scolds. "Stop it."

"Yes ma'am." I smile, grateful for her and the way she keeps me out of my head.

She's invited some of her friends from the firm over to her place tonight, so I plan to bring her breakfast in the morning before the shop opens.

I attend to the customers absentmindedly, thoughts drifting to Emmett. He's coming over tonight when he gets off—again.

I thought I'd miss having my alone time with someone staying with me every night, but I don't. I look forward to seeing him, every single time, and that scares me. We've known each other for less than a week. I made it clear yesterday that I don't want a relationship—which is true—but knowing he could and might leave at any moment terrifies me.

I don't know how I could already be so attached to him in the few days we've spent together, but as cliché as it sounds, I feel like my soul knows his.

They say the heart wants what the heart wants, but something tells me the soul is even more powerful than the heart.

Twenty-Two

Emmett

"Detective Fisher, I need to see you in my office."
Great.

Captain Harrison does not play around. He's in his late sixties and is as mean as a snake. Everyone keeps expecting him to announce his retirement, but I think he stays around out of spite. He would scare some of the toughest drill instructors I know.

I take a deep breath and follow him into his office. It's decorated wall-to-wall with awards from his military and law enforcement careers. When I first started here I thought that being a former Marine would mean that he'd go easy, or easier, on me. But that hasn't been the case.

"Yes, sir?" I ask.

"Sit down, son."

There are two brown leather chairs in front of his desk that have seen better days. I do as he says and wait for what I know is coming next.

"How do you know Raven Jackson?" His stare is penetrating, like he can see straight through me, and I decide honesty is the best policy here.

"I met her at a bar the other night and walked her home when I grew suspicious of a man who was watching her."

Short and sweet.

"This was the night of the attack on Elliott James?" His eyebrows raise as he talks.

"Yes, sir. At the time, I did not know Miss James or that she and Raven were friends. It was all a coincidence."

"I see. So you walked Miss Jackson home from the bar, and you stayed with her?"

I shift a little in my seat. "Yes, sir. We mutually decided that I would stay the night with her." I don't tell him why or how I ended up staying, but he didn't fall off the turnip truck yesterday.

"Uh huh, and then the next morning you came into the station to learn of the incident that happened the night before, and you were unaware, at the time, that Miss James and Miss Elliott were connected?"

"That is correct. I didn't know until we were in the hospital room interviewing Miss James and Raven was there with her."

"And do you believe your...*relationship*...with Miss Jackson is interfering in your investigation in any way?"

Think fast, save this. "No, sir. In fact, I believe it is helping the investigation. I was with Raven again last night, and she received an anonymous phone call in the middle of the night. I was able to report it as soon as it happened. Also, having a relationship with Raven has given me insight I don't think we could have otherwise acquired."

"Very well. Just don't get so close to the case or this woman that it clouds your judgment or bias. If it does, I'll have to pull you off it. You're walking a thin line as it is, Fisher.

"Yes, sir. Thank you."

"That's all. Now go on and get back to work and find this son of a bitch."

I want to bolt from his office, but I keep my cool and go back to my desk. It's none of his business, but my time with Raven is not strictly related to aiding the investigation by any means.

Nevermore

If I'm being honest, even the thought of walking away from her after the case is solved pains me, and I refuse to do it unless she makes me.

Wrenn Montgomery

Twenty-Three

Raven

The day passes quickly and before I know it, it's time to close the shop up and figure out what to do about dinner. Emmett is working late, so I'm on my own until he's free. I decide on having Chinese delivered, and ordering extra so Emmett can have leftovers when he gets home.

I mean, here. Not home. This is not his home.

I tidy up the shop while I'm waiting for it to be delivered, making sure that all the books are lined up evenly on the shelves and facing the correct way. When I'd made the decision to take a break from counseling and open my own bookstore, I was terrified, but I knew it was something I had to do. It'd been my dream since I was a little girl.

Reading has always been my escape from reality, and I'd used it frequently to cope with my mother and her episodes.

A few years ago, I received a letter on my birthday. I had just turned twenty-one, and I was heading into grad school that fall. The letter was from my father, whom I've never met, but it stated that he couldn't tell me his name at that time. I almost tore it up and threw it in the trash, but for some reason I held on to it. There was no return address, and it was signed Robert Cole—an alias that led to a fruitless and never-ending search, other than a successful author by that name whose books I promptly bought and read just for the hell of it.

In fact, the one Emmett was reading the other night was the first I'd purchased. With the letter there was a check, which I refused to cash. Every month on the first, a new check would come, and I made a pretty pile out of them on my desk but never cashed them. No more letters came, only the checks in the same hefty amount each month.

By the time I had about six months' worth of checks, I could pay my entire grad school tuition, but I still refused to use the money. Whoever my "father" was, I wanted no part of his money, especially if he wouldn't even tell me his real name.

One day, when Elli was at my apartment—while Landry was in prison and I was living off of Ramen noodles, barely making rent each month—she sat down at my desk to proofread a paper for me and saw the stack of checks. I tried to explain to her why I wasn't cashing them, but she was relentless, insisting that my dad owed me this money and I should take every dollar he sent my way.

Eventually I caved and cashed them, expecting them to bounce. They didn't, and I've cashed them every month since. If it makes him feel less guilty for abandoning me then so be it. I know it's selfish. A better person would've shredded the checks and kept their dignity, but after the stint with Landry, I needed the cash, and my "father" obviously wanted me to have it.

In some part of my mind, I know I'm holding out hope that if I keep cashing them, someday there will be another letter with them, possibly revealing who he is so I can finally meet him—or at least know who he is. I know it's a stretch, but if that never happens, and he just keeps sending money, I'm going to continue taking it. Especially if it keeps my dream of owning a bookstore alive.

The loud knock at the door scares me out of my thoughts and I grab my pistol before approaching. When I see that it's just the Chinese food delivery guy, we make small talk while I sign the receipt and take the food from him. As he leaves, I lean out of the front door a tad to look at the street outside.

The same black Sedan is parked where it was yesterday, and someone is inside it.

I instantly slam the door shut and lock the bolts.

I am not going to call Emmett. I am not going to call Emmett. I am a strong, independent woman with Chinese food and a gun.

If they want to come in here, I dare them. I'll be ready for them.

I push against the false wall and take the stairs two at a time until I'm in my apartment.

I head over to the picture window in the sitting area and sit down on the window seat to eat my dinner, arranging the gray and cream pillows around me so I can stare down at the car below with my pistol in my lap.

Who is it? What do they want from me? Why are they watching my store?

I'm fine, it's okay.

I am not going to call Emmett.

I eat my food but barely taste any of it, trying to rack my brain for answers, watching for any signs of movement from the car below. I'm sure they can't see me, but I sit farther back from the window—just in case.

A little girl and her mom ride their bikes down the sidewalk, right past the car that symbolizes so much ugliness in my life right now. They pedal by without a care in the world. A few doors down, the florist on the corner is putting the bouquet displays up for the night. Life continues around me, but it feels like my world is standing still until all this is solved.

I call Emmett—only because he needs to be prepared in case he drives up and the person is still outside the bookstore.

I swear.
I don't need him.
I don't.

Twenty-Four

Emmett

Getting these calls from Raven is getting old. Not because I don't want to hear from her. I hate to admit that her voice has quickly become my favorite thing to hear. But I hate the thought of someone stalking her and me not being there to protect her.

I'm tied up at the station for another hour and I can't leave. I have to finish these reports and add them to Miss James' file. I send another officer who patrols that area to go sit outside of her apartment until I can get there.

He calls when he arrives and says that the car drove off when he pulled onto her street.

Of course.

I call Raven back and let her know, hating how scared she sounds despite trying to be brave.

The last forty-five minutes tick by and I shake my head at myself for being so anxious to get to her apartment. She's told me, in more ways than one, that she doesn't want anything serious. I can't blame her for that, considering the way her last serious relationship ended, and now this situation.

We're no closer to finding the guy from the bar. The DNA results came back with no hits. The call from the other night was traced to a track phone. Every lead we get is squashed out. I've never been so frustrated.

Eventually, I glance up at the clock and see it's two after nine, so I pack my things and head to the back entrance to walk back to my apartment to change before heading to Raven's. I'm almost to the door when I hear my name being called.

"Emmett! Hey, man. Wait up."

Alex. Wonderful.

He's just coming on shift. I should've left early.

"I don't have time to chat," I say curtly. "Do you need something?"

"Yeah, I just wanted to say…I'm just…I'm really sorry. Jenna and I—"

"Look, man, it's fine. I mean, it's not fine. You were fucking my girlfriend behind my back. I don't really care about that part, but you were my partner. I was supposed to be able to trust you with my life and you were at my home fucking my girlfriend. It is what it is. I'm really enjoying day-shift and Detective Tropp is great. I don't really have much else to say to you." I know I sound bitter and maybe a little immature, but bro code is a thing. Beyond that, LEOs have their own code to follow.

"I know, and you don't know how sorry I am. There's just something about Jenna. I know you must be torn up about losing her. I just wanted to say that I'm sorry."

I try not to grin at him. I wasn't too keen on Jenna to begin with. I would've never married her. It wasn't that serious. Plus, Raven makes Jenna look like chopped liver.

"That's quite all right, Alex. I wish you and Jenna the best. Have a great night." Smirking, I turn away and head for the door.

If he thinks Jenna is the cream of the crop, great. They deserve each other. If I hadn't met Raven maybe I would be a little more upset, but I've never met a woman who could hold a candle to Raven Jackson. I decide to skip going to my apartment and head straight to her instead.

My phone rings as I'm pulling up to her apartment. "Fisher."

"Hey, detective. This is Officer Haynes. I'm the lead on the Landry Davis investigation. Just wanted to give you a call and see if you had any questions I could answer."

"I appreciate you calling. I was attempting to see Mr. Davis in relation to a case I'm working. Do you have any leads or motives for his murder?"

He laughs, and I cringe a little at the crassness. "Oh yeah. You know he took out one of the lead gang members in town? He's had a mark on his head since the day he stepped foot in here. I'm surprised it took this long. There'd been a few attempts. He was in protective custody for two years, but he'd been back in general population for six months with no problem until the fight that got him killed. We're not sure who's responsible yet, but someone will claim it before long. If it's gang related, they'll want it known that they're responsible for taking him out. And if it's not, someone will rat soon."

"Thank you for the information. I assume you've contacted his parents?"

"Of course. It's standard procedure to contact the next of kin, as you know. The mother was distraught, as expected. The father is threatening to sue, also as expected. He's a big wig attorney and has made a name for himself by turning small lawsuits into multi-million-dollar payouts. The guy's a real peach."

I bank this information away for later and thank him for his time.

We can mark Landry off the list of suspects, but I still have to tell Raven about his death.

Twenty-Five

Raven

I bite my lip as I look out my window again. It's comforting knowing an officer is here and watching until Emmett arrives.

Something about that sedan is so familiar to me. I wonder how often they've been outside of the bookstore and I didn't notice. Or I noticed and assumed they were waiting for someone else.

I've got to get better at paying attention to my surroundings. My mom used to chide me for that when I was young, before she spent more time in her drug-induced stupors than out of them.

"Your head is always in the clouds, Raven. One day you're going to have to come down and get to know the world."

I thought by becoming a counselor, I would get to know the world. Apparently not well enough.

I'm still sitting by the windowsill, my Chinese food long grown cold, when I see Emmett pull up to the store. I watch as he emerges from the car, all six-foot-three of him. Long legs, confident stride. Something about him is so different than any man I've ever known. I mean, I've always found tall men attractive, but I don't know if I've ever been so attracted to someone before.

I can't even imagine how I'd be handling this situation if I didn't have him to distract me and protect me from whatever it is that's going on. And maybe that's not a healthy coping mechanism but it sure is helping, and right now that's all I'm concerned about.

I rush down the stairs to unlock the door for him.

As soon as he's over the threshold I slam the door closed and jump into his arms.

"Well hey, gorgeous. Happy to see me?"

"Shut up." I kiss him and his hands grip my ass to hoist me up higher.

He's already heading to the staircase, wasting no time, just how I want it.

"You going to carry me up the stairs like this, Casanova?" I manage between kisses.

"Yep." His voice is low, almost a growl, and I'm not about to argue with him.

It's sexy as hell that he's so strong and can lift me like I weigh twenty pounds. He carries me up the stairs with ease and makes his way over to my bed, slow and steady, laying me down and coming to lean above me.

"I missed you," he says.

My skin tingles and I try to accept his words without the panic that's threatening to bubble over.

It's good that he missed you, Raven. You missed him, too. It doesn't mean he's trying to marry you. Tell him you missed him back.

"Oh, really?" *I can't do it. I can't tell him how much I miss him all day when he's not here. I've known him for less than a week and this is ridiculous. You can't catch feelings for someone in less than a week.*

That's enough talking and thinking for right now.

I push him over and onto his back then climb on top of him, straddling him. In seconds my shirt is off and somewhere across the room, his hands exploring every bit of exposed flesh. I reach behind myself and unhook my bra, then toss it across the room. I keep eye contact with him while I start unbuttoning my jeans. He's rock-hard beneath me, and his hips buck every time I move like he can't wait to be inside me. As much as I want to tease him and let this go slowly, I can't wait. Maybe later tonight.

I roll off of him and slide my jeans off before starting on his buckle, but he takes over and removes his jeans and boxers. He moves to push me back onto the bed again but I don't let him. Instead I push him back and kiss down his chest and abdomen.

He knows where I'm heading, and he leans back against the pillows to watch me with hooded eyes. When I reach his cock, I wrap my hands around the base and take him deep into my mouth in one fluid movement.

"Fuck," he says, breathing out, and I flash him a grin before doing it again.

I move to take him deep into my mouth once more but he grabs me by my arms and pulls me over him, flipping me over and settling between my thighs.

"Damn, Raven. I need to be inside you."

"So get a move on," I tell him.

He chuckles, and I see the glint in his eye as he grabs a condom from the nightstand, puts it on, and slides into me with a gentle thrust.

I need more. I need harder and faster and I need to come like only he can make me come. I grind my hips against him. "Move, Emmett. Please."

"Oh, like this?" He moves half an inch out and then back in. Not nearly enough.

"I swear to God, if you don't get this show on the road and fuck me—"

"Like this?" He pulls out and slams back into me, again and again.

I moan. "Exactly. Exactly like that."

Wrenn Montgomery

Twenty-Six

Emmett

Lying beside Raven in the dark, I feel like I can finally breathe.

I wasn't expecting her to jump me like she did, but I'm not complaining.

I need to update her on the investigation—which would be a hell of a lot easier if I had any leads—and more importantly, Landry's death. I start with offering what I do know.

"Officer Lane described the sedan he saw to me. I think it was the same, plates and all," I say, testing the waters.

"Yeah," she agrees.

"Would you feel more comfortable staying somewhere else? With Elli? With me?" I know the answer before I finish the question, but I have to try.

"Nope."

"I'm just saying whoever is behind this knows where you live. I'm not sure this is the safest—"

"I know what you're saying, but I'm not leaving. And while I appreciate you being here to keep me company, I don't need you to do that either."

We both know that's a lie, but the way she turns her face away from me tells me that she doesn't want me to call her on it, so I don't. "I know I don't have to. I want to. I like spending time with you. I like waking up with you and coming home—"

"Just stop there. I enjoy those things, too. But you cannot get attached. I don't know what this is but I know what it isn't, and I've been honest with you from the beginning. I don't want a relationship, with you or with anyone for that matter. I don't plan on ever getting married. I don't want kids. I don't want attachments."

Call me delusional, but I don't believe any of that. I know she's guarded, and I understand why. When we catch the perp and this whole thing is over, my next mission is to start knocking down those walls of hers.

"There's something else I need to tell you," I say, changing the topic back to what's more important right now.

Her annoyance fades as she realizes that I'm serious. "What is it?"

"I went to see Landry in prison—"

"What?!"

"He was killed three weeks ago. Someone stabbed him in a fight that broke out in the yard. I'm sorry, Raven. I'm not sure if—"

"Oh my God. *Oh* my *God*!" she repeats.

I let her freak out for a second, unsure if I should hold her or grant her the space she probably wants. I settle for putting my hand on her shoulder.

She's quiet for a few minutes, staring down at her hands.

I give her the time to let her deal with whatever she's feeling.

"They didn't even call me. They didn't even tell me," she says, still looking down.

"I'm sorry." I don't know what else to say, so I rub circles on her shoulder blade.

"I'm okay. I'm sorry for freaking out. I just can't believe...but of course. I mean, he *did* kill a fucking gang member. Surely this was always a possibility, but his parents, maybe they blame me. They've been dealing with a lot I'm sure. They've probably already had the service," she says, rambling on as I keep rubbing her back and shoulders, unsure what she needs from me but wanting to help.

She reaches for her phone, and I listen while she tells Elli what I just told her. I'm close enough to hear that Elli isn't as shocked or upset as Raven is, but she does try to comfort her friend before they hang up.

Raven puts her phone down and takes a deep breath. "I'm fine I promise. It surprised me, and I'm not sure how to feel about it, but I'm okay. Thank you for telling me."

I nod and lie down, pulling her to my chest. "It's normal to feel sad, or upset, or angry. However you feel, it's normal."

Her shoulders shake and I think she's crying, but then a sudden giggle bursts out of her. "Are you the counselor? Or am I?" She laughs again and rolls onto her back, looks up at the ceiling, then takes a deep breath as she snuggles into my side.

We lie that way for a few minutes, until I hear a vibrating noise coming from my pants on the floor. I reluctantly remove Raven's leg from across my waist and roll out of her bed, looking back at her beautiful still-naked body while I search my pockets for my phone.

Once I find it, I pick up and say, "Detective Fisher."

"Fisher, it's Alex again. We just had someone call in and say they know who attacked Elliott James. Pence and Lane are heading there to take her statement. I thought you'd want to know."

"Okay, thanks for the info." I hang up.

I'm going to have to work with Alex for the foreseeable future, so as much as it pains me I'm going to have to learn how to deal with him from time to time.

"Everything okay?" Raven's voice is sleepy, like she's close to drifting off, probably exhausted from the emotional rollercoaster we just went on.

"Yeah, gorgeous. Everything is fine." I'll tell her in the morning. She needs her sleep, and this will just get her anxious all over again. "I've got to head out to a lead. Are you sure you're all right here?"

Please, God, don't let this be a case of mistaken identity or a false lead.

If I'm leaving her naked in bed it better be for a damn good reason, especially after just giving her news like that. Plus, we could really use a break in the case.

"Mm hmm," she mumbles.

I'm pretty sure she's already asleep, but I lean down and plant a kiss on her forehead anyway before taking off and locking up.

I call an officer to come sit outside of her building until I can come back.

Just in case.

Twenty-Seven

Raven

My alarm clock goes off on my iPhone and I shut it off, rolling back over to an empty bed. It feels strange now that I've gotten used to waking up with Emmett. I check my phone and see I have a text from him to call him when I wake up.

I don't.

I need some distance.

I tried again last night to explain that I don't want a relationship with him, because I know that I don't. But I also don't want to lose whatever we have going on, and I need to sort out what that means.

And the bomb he dropped about Landry…

I'm not sure how I feel about that. I feel guilty for putting him in jail, but I know that's not valid or accurate. I feel guilty for being relieved that he's really gone and not behind this. But I'm sad for his parents. Having their only child go to prison must have been hard, but burying him must have been beyond devastating.

I take a second to try to collect myself. I have another few hours before the shop opens, and one of my actually-dependable employees is opening for me, so I take the extra time to try to sort out my feelings.

When I'm avoiding my feelings I usually read, and as tempting as that is I know I need to address this, so I run a bath instead. My bathroom is my safe haven, as strange as that sounds. It's all white and gray, no color to be seen, and something about that always calms me down. Neutrals are safe.

I peruse my selection of bubble baths, beads, and oils and decide I need something relaxing, so I grab the lavender scented bath oil and dump a good amount in. Making sure my fluffy white towel is in reach, I step in, letting my feet and legs adjust before sliding down into the warm water. I know the running joke is that women love water that just about scorches their skin off, but that's never been me. Give me a little warmer than lukewarm and we're good to go.

As I sink down into the water I lean my head back on the bath pillow and close my eyes. I left my cell phone out in the loft so I could focus, after texting Elli that I would be out of reach for a few and if she needed me for an emergency to have Misty run down here and let me know. I know she won't, though. She knows how I get when I'm overwhelmed and how much I value alone time.

Okay, Raven, let's start with the basics.

I think, reverting back to my counselor ways and treating myself as a patient. Just facts and no feelings.

His name is Emmett Fisher, he's a former Marine and a detective.

You've known him since Friday, and today is Tuesday, so that's five whole days.

You haven't spent a night away from him since that first night.

What do I know about him?

He was shot in combat, medically retired, and is now in law enforcement. He has two brothers and had a difficult childhood. He just recently—as in, five days ago—ended his relationship with his current girlfriend after catching his partner screwing her. So potentially, I'm a rebound, though he says that's not the case. But don't they all?

What does he know about me?

He knows about Elli, Landry, and my mom. He knows about my dad leaving. He doesn't know the ins and outs of that situation or about the checks that come every month. He knows I have a counseling degree, but he hasn't asked why I'm not counseling anymore. He seems to appreciate the bookstore, and he's a bookworm, too. Check plus in that column.

Logically, knowing someone for only five days and having feelings for them seems completely ridiculous. Even though they say you can fall in love the first time you see someone, I've never been one to believe in that. Love takes work. It doesn't just happen overnight like it does in the movies. Love takes two people working toward the same goal together, over and over, until it works.

Would I want to work side by side with Emmett toward that goal?

I can see it. I can see loving him.

As foolish as it sounds, I can see me wanting to put that work in and have a life with him. The problem would come if/when he doesn't want to put the same amount of work in.

The worst problem comes when you've been putting in your side of the work to find out that they've quit their "job" and never turned in a notice to you—*ahem, Landry.*

I know that Emmett is nothing like Landry. On paper they're night and day. Their personalities couldn't be more opposite.

What am I really, truly scared of?

The commitment? Losing him?

If I shut him out I'm going to inevitably lose him anyway. That's a foolish reason to walk away from the first person that's made me feel something in five years.

Is five years long enough of a cool-down period to feel like I can trust someone again?

I don't know.

I promised myself I'd never trust anyone again. I know that's dramatic, but it's true.

Could I go back on that promise to myself?

Could I trust Emmett?

I don't know.

But the only way to find out is to find out.

By the time I'm pruned up and the water is cool, I've decided the best course of action is slow and steady. I'm going to give Emmett a chance, but I'm going to stay cautious, as always. I'll keep a close check on my feelings and rein them in when needed.

I can do this.

I can let someone in.

I climb out of the bath and get dressed for the day, then I do my hair and makeup for the first time since Friday night. I can't help but notice how refreshed my reflection looks. There's a glint in my eyes and my face isn't quite as "resting bitch face" as normal.

Sleeping beside Emmett every night has its perks, I guess.

Twenty-Eight

Emmett

I hated that I didn't get to go back to bed with Raven last night. The lead took longer than we thought, and even though it was the middle of the night, we had to investigate it as soon as we could.

The witness had apparently seen our suspect going back to his room on Friday night and noticed blood on his shoes and pants. She thought it was strange, so she had told someone at the front desk, who didn't report it, and she didn't know what else to do. When she saw the sketch that Elli had worked on with the sketch artist last night on the eleven o'clock news, she recognized him right away and called it in.

We headed straight to the hotel after receiving the tip, but the front desk clerk said the suspect hadn't been there all day, though he was still checked into the hotel. They told us they would let us know as soon as they saw him return to his room.

We could then pick him up for questioning, but we'd have to either locate those bloody clothes or get some sort of confession out of him to keep him at the station.

Detective Tropp puts her desk phone back into its cradle and turns to me. "Hotel desk confirmed he's there now. Let's go."

Holstering my gun as we hit the stairs, I say a prayer that this goes smoothly and we catch this bastard.

I need Raven to feel safe—from this threat, and with me.

"Jonestown Police. Open up!"

The officer to my right nods at me to put the key card in the door. I do so and two officers from behind me rush forward as they burst into the hotel room.

"Clear," I hear, and my heart falls as Tropp and I proceed into the room.

Our suspect is nowhere to be found, but there's a plate of half-eaten food on the bed and the TV is on, making me think he must've gotten wind that we were on the way and bailed. In the corner of the room there are some balled up clothes, so we take them for processing and start going through the drawers and the two duffle bags on the desk.

"There's not much in here, Em." Tropp's disappointment laces her voice and I feel it, too.

I'm hopeful that we can at least get some DNA from the utensils he was using. We also take his toothbrush and comb. If we can match this to the blood found at Elli's apartment, we'll have proof this is our guy.

"Wait, over here," I hear another officer call out, and he pulls something out from under the mattress.

It's a file folder with Raven's name on the outside, and my heart drops.

Inside, there are photos of her, a paper with her description, places she visits frequently and where she orders takeout food from, the address of her bookstore, her mother's name, information about Elli and the owners of the coffee shop around the corner…the list goes on and on.

"What the hell?" Tropp asks as she and I exchange looks. "So this was a hit on Raven, then?"

I nod. I can feel my jaw clenching at the thought of some creep having all this personal information on Raven.

"Do you need a minute, detective?" she asks low, so none of the other officers can hear.

I appreciate the thoughtfulness, grateful that we've already had the talk about how close I've gotten to this case. "No, I'm fine, thanks. Let's log all of this and get back to the department. Have an officer stay here and wait to see if the asshole comes back. I doubt he will now that he's been compromised, but he may need this information."

The sick feeling in my stomach won't fade and I know I have to get a handle on this before I'm pulled from the case.

How the hell do they know so much about her?

Someone has been tailing her for a while, or someone in her life is only close to her to feed information to whoever is behind this. I'm leaning toward the latter, and I need to find out who before they get to her.

Wrenn Montgomery

Twenty-Nine

Raven

I bound down the stairs and slip through the hidden doorway, relieved to find no customers lurking close enough to have seen me.

Reggie, my most faithful employee, is behind the desk working his magic. I hear him telling the group of giggling girls in front of him all the best romances that we currently have in stock. They're hanging on his every word, and I can see why. He's tall, athletic, and handsome, but he has that total hot nerd thing going on. He's wearing a vintage Beatles tee—a real one, not a remake from *Hot Topic*—and skinny jeans that fit him just right. His caramel colored skin is complemented by a pair of striking chocolate colored eyes and his dark-rimmed glasses fit him perfectly. He's a looker for sure.

Unfortunately for those girls, he's also as gay as they come and has been in a committed relationship with his partner for three years.

I shoot him a wink over their heads as I go to check the stock, straightening books as I go.

When the last of the giggling gaggle exit the stop, he lets out a sigh of relief and I can't help but burst out laughing.

"What? I just sold seven new releases, thank you very much!" he says.

This only makes me laugh harder and I high-five him as he makes his way over the shelf I'm working on. "Thank God you're back. You can't take any more vacations. I can barely run this place without you." I nudge his shoulder with mock sternness and he rolls his eyes.

"I was gone one weekend. You did fine."

"You have no idea. This weekend was hell." I quickly give him a breakdown of the events that have occurred since he left and by the end of my story his mouth is hanging open.

"Shut the front door! Raven! You should've called. I would've come back earlier!"

"No! No way. You needed that break away with Todd. I handled it. Oh, and I also fired Lacey."

"About freaking time. She always creeped me out."

I tilt my head, surprised by this. "How so?"

"IDK. I always got the vibe she was a little obsessed with you."

"Quit speaking in abbreviations," I tell him. "I think she was just lonely or flighty or something."

"IDK. Either way, I'm glad she's gone."

I roll my eyes at his obvious disregard for grammar and let it go. "I keep thinking she's going to show up to get her check, but she hasn't yet. It's in the top drawer of the front desk, if she comes in when I'm not here."

"Yes ma'am. Okay, now…Emmett. Tell me more about him again? What's he look like?"

I shake my head and launch into a detailed description of my hunky detective that has Reggie drooling and me dying of laughter by the end of it. We're so wrapped up in our conversation that I don't hear the bell over the door until Reggie nudges me and motions for me to look.

We're still in the back of the room, hidden by the shelves, and there's only one lone customer up front.

Nevermore

I peak between the shelves instead of calling out like I normally do, and thank God for that, because the creep from the bar—and Elli's suspected rapist—is standing in the doorway of my shop.

Thirty

Emmett

The car ride back to the department was tense. I was so thankful that Monica was driving so I could take a minute to collect myself.

We'd assumed that Raven was the hit since she had gotten the letter and the phone call, but seeing it on paper like that made it all come to a head for me. They even know her mother's name, even though Raven cut ties with her years ago.

Who would know those facts about her?

Someone's been feeding them information, but who?

I need to address this with Raven, but I know it's going to freak her out. It would make anyone uneasy knowing that someone you don't know has that much information on you. It's even worse when your best friend has been attacked and you know you were the intended target.

"You all right?" Monica's look of concern washes over me and I pull it together.

"Yeah, we've just got to find him. How did he get out of the hotel that fast? We even had officers at the back and side entrances, just in case, and no one spotted him. None of the security cameras show him leaving."

"I was thinking about that. Do you think he had another room? An adjoining one? Maybe one down the hall? Or he could have an accomplice and he slipped into their room…"

"That's possible. The clerk said there was only one room registered to Brent Smallwood but it could be under another name. Why don't they have cameras in the damn hallways?" I groan and rub my hands on my face.

"We're going to catch him, Fisher. But you have to pull yourself together before word of how distraught you are gets back to captain and he takes you off the case."

I know she's right, so I nod and count to ten in my head.

We're pulling up the station now and I need to put on a good show. It's okay to act concerned, it's not okay to act like I'm losing my mind—or rush home to Raven to never leave her side again.

She still hasn't responded to my text from this morning, which is odd. I try to call her cell when I get back to my desk, but she doesn't answer.

Probably busy at the shop. It is the middle of the afternoon.

I can't wait to get off work and go to her, but I have five hours left. I sit down to do my reports on today, trying to clear my mind and focus on the facts.

My cell phone starts ringing and I smile when I see the number that comes across. "Hey, babe. Having a good day?"

"Uh, hi. This is Reggie. I, uh, I work for Raven. I don't know why I called you and not 911. I'm an idiot. I saw your number and—"

I sit up and ask, "Wait, what do you mean? Is everything okay? Where is Raven?"

I hear a sob on the other end of the line and I'm already running down the stairs, Tropp following behind me, when Reggie says, "He took her."

Thirty-One

Raven

"You're a fucking idiot," I grumble to myself as I try to sit up and take in my surroundings.

I have no idea where I am.

Deep breaths, Raven. Panicking isn't going to help you right now. Use your head and be smart.

I look around the room. I'm lying on a comfortable bed, fully clothed in what I was wearing this morning.

It's dark outside. I can see through the window across the room, but there's a lamp on the bedside table that's been turned on. The walls are shades of gray, with touches of blue here and there. The furniture is white wicker and there's a painting of a gray sky with thunder clouds over the ocean above the bed.

It's the perfect beach house room. Definitely not your typical kidnapping scenario.

Who kidnaps someone and puts them in a guest room?

I test out my limbs and find I'm not shackled. I'm willing to bet the door is also unlocked.

What the hell?

I sit up and my head is woozy, but I seem to be otherwise unharmed. On the nightstand beside the lamp there's a glass of water, what appears to be an Aspirin, and a note that reads:

Raven,

It's not what you think. Come downstairs when you're ready and I'll explain.

RC

I shake my head and stare at the note.

Who the fuck is RC?

Robert Cole.

The thought hits me like a ton of bricks and I have to talk myself out of an actual panic attack for the first time in years.

Breathe, Raven, breathe. Your father would not have your best friend raped and beaten. There's no way this is the same RC.

Who else could it be, though? That's exactly how the letter was signed. It's him.

When I'm calmed down enough, I stand up and test my weight, steadying myself. I think of drinking the water and taking the Aspirin but I'm hesitant. I'm not trying to get drugged again.

I head over to the door and turn the knob, which of course isn't locked. It creaks open and I curse. I was hoping to have the element of surprise when I met my kidnapper.

So much for that.

"Raven?" a man's voice calls from below, and I shudder.

Time to face the music, sweet pea. You got yourself in this and you'll find a way out.

I start down the stairs carefully, unsure of what's going to be waiting for me at the bottom.

When I reach the last step, I see a tall thin man with salt and pepper hair standing in a modern and large kitchen.

"Raven."

There are tears in his eyes and I immediately hate him. This is what I do. When people show emotion I shut down and turn their emotions against them.

"It's clear that you know my name. Care to do me the favor of telling me who you are?" I say.

"I see your fiery spirit hasn't changed."

A sinking feeling in my gut tells me what I need to know. Those eyes, they're my eyes. That's where I got them. The sharpness of his chin is the same as mine. I'm assuming his salt and pepper hair was jet black a few years ago, also just like mine.

"So you're my father, then."

"I am."

I stare at him a few more seconds, the rage building.

"I'd love to talk with you, to get to know—"

"Did you kidnap me?" I cross the room and I'm in his face in seconds.

What the hell is wrong with my fight or flight instincts? Flight, Raven. Flight.

He starts to shake his head and I interrupt him before he can talk.

"Because from where I'm standing, someone attacked my best friend, sent me a threatening letter, has been casing my store, and then suddenly shows up at my store and the next thing I know I'm drugged and somehow wind up here with you." By the end of my rant, my voice has reached a new octave I didn't know I had.

"Whoa, hang on, Raven. I swear I don't know what you're talking about. I can see how this is confusing, but I didn't kidnap you. I saved you."

Thirty-Two

Emmett

Blue lights and frantic noise surround Raven's store, an echoing of the sickness in the pit of my stomach.

When we first got here, there had been what appeared to be a wreck out front. One car is still on the scene, completely demolished. The driver is gone, a blood trail stopping around the corner where he must have been picked up by another vehicle.

We have an alert out at every local hospital to call us if someone has related injuries.

Reggie was inside Poe's at the time, along with the lone customer who had called 911. Both of their statements had been taken, both of them saying that Raven had walked right up to the man who entered—the man we assume was Brent Smallwood.

He then grabbed her and she went limp as he carried her out over his shoulder and put her into his car, which was then hit head first by the other vehicle. We think Brent got away on foot. The other vehicle was not as damaged and drove off, after securing Raven and putting her in *their* car. This entire thing is a nightmare, and none of it makes sense.

I'm taking a little solace in the fact that it doesn't appear as though Raven is currently with Brent, but nonetheless, she has been kidnapped and right now we have no idea who this other party is.

"I know you're worrying yourself sick and it's understandable, but you've got to pull it together so we can find her and you don't get yourself jerked off this case," Monica says to me under her breath, the voice of reason.

I nod at her and make a note to buy her coffee for an entire month after this is over to thank her for being so supportive during this whole ordeal. She could just as easily rat me out to the captain and tell him how this is affecting me.

"We're having the tech department see if they can get a visual on the car that Raven was put in from any of the traffic cameras. That's really all we can do right now, until someone gets a lead on the APB we put out. Why don't you go home and try to rest? We need you at your best for this, Em."

I know she's right but the thought of going home and doing nothing makes me want to hit something. "I'm going to stay here a little longer, in case anything turns up. You go ahead, though. I'll be heading home soon. I promise."

At this point we are both on our second hour of overtime. I should be curled up with Raven in her bed right now, not pacing her store and trying to rack my brain for who could have snatched her.

Monica nods and heads out with the last of the officers and crime scene investigators, leaving me alone in the shop.

Reggie left an hour or so ago, thoroughly shaken up. His partner had come to pick him up and seemed to be doing a decent job of calming him down so hopefully he can get some rest tonight. I'm sure there will be more questioning tomorrow.

I sigh and look around trying to think.

Who would kidnap Raven? Other than this Brent Smallwood.

Who is she estranged from?

She said her mother is into drugs; it could be one of her dealers who found out she has a daughter. I make a note to get in contact with the mother tomorrow. She'll take some tracking down but we need to rule out every option.

She hasn't seen her father since she was a baby, so that's out.

No other ex-boyfriends except the one who's now deceased.

I need more to go on. I don't want to snoop through her things—it's a violation of privacy and a line I don't want to cross—but I need to think like a detective and not like a lover. And a detective would be going through her things, looking for clues on who would do this to her.

I start with her desk downstairs in the main room of the shop, but I don't find anything of any value. Just receipt records, a wish-list of books she wants to order for the shop, future goals she has for her business, and things like that.

I move to the storage room, but all I find there are books waiting to be stocked, extra T-shirts with a cartoon Raven—the bird, not my girl—and a swirly handwriting font advertising Poe's.

I know I need to head upstairs. Anything personal would be up there. Raven is too private to have anything of importance down here.

I reveal the hidden staircase and head up the steps, her scent hitting me as I reach the loft. My vision swims and actual tears form in my eyes.

Jesus, Fisher.

I'm so worried about her I could puke. Whoever took her stole her from a harmful kidnapper. I can only hope they won't harm her and were simply saving her.

But if that's the case, why hasn't she called?

Heading over to the desk in the corner, I try the drawers. One is locked and another opens easily. The one that opens has nothing interesting, just some notebooks and a few novels she's stashed there with bookmarks in the pages.

One of which is the book I was reading on her sofa a few nights ago. When I flip it over a sense of familiarity rushes over me. The symbol on the back cover is the same Celtic knot the guy from the car had tattooed on his forearm.

Could this just be a coincidence?

The author is R. Cole. I pull out my phone and take a photo of the front and back of the book, storing it away for future reference.

I feel around in the drawer, knowing Raven wouldn't be the type to store a key inside an unlocked drawer.

Where else would it be? Think, Emmett, think…

I check all the potted plants. Walking over to the windowsill I lift them one by one, until I find a tiny key under one.

Smart girl.

Rushing back over to the desk, I unlock the drawer and pull it all the way out. Sitting down on the floor, I begin to empty the contents one by one. There's a letter addressed to Raven, a photo of a dark-haired baby in the arms of a red-headed woman and a dark-haired man with a striking resemblance to Raven.

They must be her parents.

Underneath those are a pile of check stubs and deposit slips. All of them in huge amounts of money, starting almost five years ago.

Who is sending her this much money? Landry's family? Is it hush money?

I go back to the letter and open it, trying not to feel guilty for reading something I really have no business reading. But if it helps us find her, it's worth the wrath I'm going to receive.

Raven,

I know you don't know me, and I know you may not want to. I wish I could tell you my real name, but I can't yet.

I promise you, one day I will explain everything. I am your father, but for now, you can call me Robert Cole.

Nothing can replace the years that I have missed out on with you. Nothing will ever make up for me leaving you when I did. Please know that I have always loved you. I have watched you from afar for a while, trying to learn about you and your life here.

I'm so proud of you for everything you have already accomplished, and I know you will accomplish so much more.

I have enclosed a check. If you're anything like your mother, I know you won't want to cash it. Please do, Raven. It's the very least I can do. I know college isn't cheap, and I hate that you've taken this burden upon yourself. I will continue sending checks every month. Please take them and allow them to provide security to you. I know it doesn't make up for anything, but at least I'll know you're financially taken care of.

Love you always,
RC

I put the letter down.

What in the fuck did I just read?

Raven's real dad—whose name we don't know—has been sending her money for the last five years? To make up for abandoning her?

I flip through the check stubs. She didn't cash the first check until over seven months after it came. I'm guessing she held out as long as she could before she had to use it. This would have been around the time Landry went to jail and his parents quit paying her tuition. I can imagine how much it hurt her pride to cash those checks.

A pounding on the door downstairs sets me on edge and I grab my gun, cautiously heading back down the steps.

When I turn the corner I see a very short, very bruised, very angry blonde banging away on the door and cussing worse than any Marine I've ever known.

An angry Elliott James may be *scarier* than any Marine I've ever known.

Thirty-Three

Raven

"What the fuck do you mean, you *saved* me?" I spit out, the rage still burning in my chest. I know I look angry, too. I always turn red when I'm mad and my chest and neck are on fire.

"Okay, so you don't remember anything?"

"No!" I snap. "How about you start explaining? Now." My plan to go with calm and collected has flown out of the window, fast.

My father rubs the space between his shoulder and his neck. "I've been watching your bookstore for a while."

"Oh so that's been you then? The creeper in the black sedan out front? Nice." The sarcasm is so thick you could reach out and dip your hand in it.

"Yes, Raven, that was me." He at least has the gall to look sheepish. "I was parked half a block down this evening when I saw a man enter the shop. Something about him didn't sit right with me, and I drove a little closer up to get a better view through the windows out front."

"Brent," I state.

"Excuse me?"

I roll my eyes, which is petty because this isn't really his fault, but the entire situation is pissing me off and I think I have a right to be snarky. "Brent Smallwood. He's the guy who was entering the shop. He's the one who has *also* been stalking me, and he raped my best friend this past weekend. He's the guy that drugged me." I'm wary to tell him anything else, in case he's actually working with Brent, though my gut tells me that's not the case.

"Jesus. I saw him come in and I saw you approach him. You looked defiant, like you were ready for a confrontation. When he reached out and grabbed you, I saw you go limp and my instincts took over. The second he was in his car I rammed him head on. In retrospect, I should have left it at that, but I didn't know if he had more goons with him or if someone else would be coming along, so I grabbed you, put you in my car, and drove us here," he finishes, watching me cautiously like he's not sure if I'm a bomb about to go off.

He's smarter than I've given him credit for all these years.

"So you kidnapped me…from a kidnapper…"

He rubs his hands over his face and says, "Essentially, yes."

"Can I make a phone call? Because I'm sure you've caused quite a ruckus and I need to let everyone know I'm okay."

"Yes, absolutely." He jumps up and grabs his phone from the table beside the couch. "You didn't have yours when I grabbed you…er…saved you…"

I almost chuckle at how awkward he is.

Guess I got that from him.

I grab the phone he's extending to me, my anger dissolving little by little. I don't remember anyone's phone numbers.

Damn technology.

The time says it's close to midnight, so if I call the bookstore no one is going to answer. I use his phone to google the Jonestown PD phone number.

"Detective Sams," a man answers.

"Hello, this is Raven Jackson—"

"Raven Jackson? The kidnapping victim?"

"Um, yeah that's me. I just wanted to let everyone know that I'm all safe. I don't have my phone, I couldn't call Emm—uh, Detective Fisher—and I wasn't sure what else to do."

"Oh thank God, he's been worried sick. We all have. Where are you? Are you hurt?"

"No, I'm okay. It appears that the real kidnapper was hit by my father. He grabbed me trying to save me from more potential kidnappers and I'm at his beach house in…" I look over at my father, having no idea where we are.

"Carolina Beach, two-eight-nine-three Magnolia Lane."

I relay the information to Detective Sams and he says they'll send someone out to check on me, legally unable to take my word for my well-being. He promises he'll let Emmett know that I'm all right, and I ask him to please also call Elliott James, to which he agrees and says someone should be here in a few hours to interview me and take me back home.

I hang up and look over at my dad, unsure if I can even call him that. "We have a few hours. Now would be a good time for you to explain where the fuck you've been and why you've been stalking me from afar."

He nods. "Can I get you some coffee? You'll probably need it."

Wrenn Montgomery

Thirty-Four

Emmett

I see Elliott standing outside of the bookstore, and if looks could kill I would be dead.

I unlock the door and step back, giving her a wide berth. Her hands are flailing and I can't understand her through the cursing and high-pitch squeal of her voice.

"And you motherfuckers didn't even think to call me? *Me*?! Her best fucking friend?? No one is going to let her best friend know that she's been fucking *kidnapped*? And you of all people should have known to call me! I will have your goddamn head and your goddamn job!"

"Elli…Miss James…please calm down and let me explain—"

"Miss James! And what could you possibly say that could explain this? My best friend has been *kidnapped* and no one could be bothered to let me know? I had to find out from a frantic Reggie!"

"Okay, if you calm down I'll tell you what we know, but I can't speak to you when you're acting like this. You're a lawyer, you know how this process works." I try to rationalize with her, knowing it's a gamble and she's either going to actually calm down so we can have a conversation, or she's going to shove my balls down my throat like she's been threatening to do.

She takes not one, not two, but five deep breaths in a row with her eyes tightly shut. "Okay, I'm calm. Please, Detective Fisher, would you mind telling me what the hell is going on?"

I know the calmness is a façade, but I'll take it.

I tell her everything we know, her eyes growing bigger and then squinting into barely-there slits when I tell her about the second kidnapper.

"And who the fuck was that?" she asks.

"We have no idea. Do you know of anyone else that would do this?"

She worries her lip while she thinks, but then shakes her head. "No, honestly. Raven isn't the friendliest person in the world, but she wouldn't hurt a fly and I don't know anyone who doesn't love her once they get to know her. She doesn't have any enemies that I know of."

I don't want to ask but I have to. "What about her dad?"

"What do you mean? She doesn't have a relationship with him."

"I know about the checks," I say, coming clean.

"Oh, yeah, she's been getting them for a few years now. I had to convince her to cash them, but as far as I know that's the only contact they've ever had, aside from the letter he sent with the first one."

I nod, that being pretty much what I expected. We stand there for a few minutes, both of us lost in thought. The ring of my cell phone breaks the silence and I lunge for it, checking the caller ID.

Fucking Alex.

"Fisher," I answer.

"We've found her. Or rather, she called in. She's safe. She's with her father in Carolina Beach. We have officers on the way now to—"

"No, I'm going down there." I start gathering my things and motion for Elli to come with me, relief flooding through me at the knowledge of her being safe.

"The captain specifically asked that you stay, but I can cover for you and say you didn't know and headed down anyway."

"And why would you do that?" I ask him.

"I fucked up and betrayed your trust, Emmett. I know I fucked up. Let me try to fix it. Go. I won't say a word. If anyone asks, she called you, too. I'll text you the address."

I pause, trying to decide if I can trust him after what we've been through this last week, and ultimately decide I don't care. If he tells the captain, so be it. I'm going to her.

"Thanks. I'll keep you updated on her status. I need to go now if I'm going to beat the other officers there." We hang up and I turn to Elli. "She's with her dad. It doesn't make much sense but I'm relieved nonetheless. They're in Carolina Beach. You coming with?"

"Fuck yes I'm coming with."

"Let's roll then."

Wrenn Montgomery

Thirty-Five

Raven

"So go ahead and explain it all to me." The sarcasm in my voice is still thick, but I do want to know what has kept this man away from me my entire life.

He takes a deep breath and I see regret in his eyes.

This should be good.

"When I met your mother, she was my secretary," he starts.

I let out a small chuckle in disbelief.

Of course she was.

"On paper, we had an affair. In reality, I was head over heels in love with her. She was perfect. Witty, sarcastic, fiery, beautiful…everything I'd ever wanted. I know this isn't going to change the way you feel about me, and I have to accept that, but please know you were never unwanted, Raven. I was already married when I met your mother. We have two children, two sons, so you have two half-brothers. Until about six months ago, they didn't know about you and neither did their mother. When your mother found out she was pregnant with you, she cut me off. She told me I had to choose between my wife and sons, or a life with you and her.

I wish like hell that I could say I was strong enough to walk away from my life to be with you and your mom, but

I wasn't. My wife's family owned the company I worked for. I knew that if I divorced her or told her about the affair, I would lose my family and my career.

I'm not proud of my choices. I thought about you every single day of your life. I begged your mother to stay on at the company so I could help her. I asked her to send me photos of you. I offered to help her financially. She wouldn't hear any of it. She let me see you twice after you were born, and then one day she was just gone.

She left with you and it took me years to track you down. I know I deserved that. I know why she left. But it was hell not knowing where you were and if you were okay. I figured she had met someone else and gotten married, maybe found a job in another state.

When I finally found you again, you were twelve. I sent a letter to her and asked that she please let me meet with you, or at least let me send you a letter. There was no answer, and the next letter I sent was returned to sender. You were gone again. I hired a private investigator, with no luck. I didn't find you again until you enrolled in college. That's when I started sending you the checks.

I always wanted to be a part of your life, Raven. I haven't gone about it the right way, and I lived a lie for many years, but you were always important to me. I know your mother's intentions were good. She didn't want you to grow up feeling like you were my little secret, or that you were second-best to my family with Sarah. And she was probably right to move away with you. I hope you can forgive me, or at the very least, not hate me."

I shake my head. I should've known that it was something like this. He had chosen his other family and cushy job over me and my mom. That should probably enrage me. I should be yelling at him right now, upset that I *was* second-best to his family. But I'm not. Maybe it's the psychology background, maybe it's just that I'm too old to care. I'm sad that he got himself into this situation, and I'm sad for my mom. But I can see why he did what he did. I'm a little hurt, and while I won't go running into his arms, I understand.

"You're an author, aren't you?" I finally reply.

"Yes, I write under the same name I sign your checks with," he says, sadness still in his eyes.

"Robert Cole," I mutter.

"Yes. Writing has always been my outlet, just like it appears that books have become yours."

"So you did write *The Widow's Walk.*" It's a statement. I know my favorite book has the same pen name as my father's checks. I found it when I was Googling him, trying to figure out who he could be.

"Yep, that's one of mine."

"I thought so. And your tattoo," I say, nodding toward the Celtic knot on his forearm, "for Mom?"

He nods, tears brimming his eyes. "I know you probably think it's silly, to love someone this much after all this time, but I truly believe she was my soulmate. How is she?"

I stare up at the ceiling. There are wooden beams that contrast the white beautifully, and to my left there's a wall of windows with a perfect view of the ocean. It's calming here, and I can see why he chose this place. I take a deep breath.

How do you tell your father you've only just met that the love of his life, your mother, turned out to be a drunk who mentally abused you for most of your life?

"Mom is…she's not well. She hasn't been for a very long time. She made a lot of bad choices…after you…decided. She's been in and out of jail for the last few years." I wait for his reaction, then look down and study the floor with intensity.

"Oh. I had no idea. I thought…I mean…I tried to find her a few times and I only found dead-ends. Houses that she used to live in, friends that weren't sure where she went or how long she'd been gone. I guess it makes sense now." His brow furrows as he looks off into the distance, and I see that this is unsettling news for him.

"I'm sorry, I wish I had more information for you," I offer. "I haven't spoken to her in years."

He nods, almost cutting me off short, a new look of determination in his eyes. "No, you don't have any reason to be sorry. *I'm* sorry. I should have done a better job of checking on you. I should've known what was going on."

"You couldn't have known." I don't know why I feel the need to comfort him—I'm still pretty sure I hate him—but I do feel sorry for him. Two parts of me are at war with each other.

He nods, like he knows feelings are hard for me. Maybe they're hard for him, too. "Anyway, I'm sorry. I can't tell you enough how much I regret not being in your life. I want to be now, if you'll let me."

I give him a shrug, not wanting to commit to anything. "We have a lot to figure out. We can take it one step at a time. There's no need to make rash decisions in highly emotional states." I know I sound like a counselor, but he gives me a small smile anyway.

There's a knock at the door, more like a pounding. I know our conversation is over, and I'm both relieved and saddened.

He stands to go let the officers in, giving me one last pain-filled look over his shoulder. We have a way to go if we're going to make any sort of relationship work.

"Raven." Emmett's voice echoes through the foyer, followed quickly by Elli's squawking.

I let out a breath I didn't know I was holding and tears come to my eyes as I stand and rush to where they are.

I grin when I hear Elli begin to give my father a thorough verbal lashing. I could go save him, but I don't.

Nevermore

Emmett wraps his arms around me and kisses the top of my head—and for a moment I forget that there's a rapist on the loose who tried to kidnap me today.

Thirty-Six

Emmett

Holding Raven in the foyer of her kidnapper/father's home brings me a peace I don't know I've ever experienced. The ache in my chest is finally subsiding, and I feel like I'm returning to my body after the last eight hours of complete hell.

I step back and hold her at arm's length, checking her over and making sure she's unharmed.

"I'm fine, I promise," she says with a chuckle, but I hear the exhaustion in her tone. It's almost two in the morning and she's been through her own hell today.

"Do you want to talk about it now or wait until we get back?" I ask under my breath, silently hoping that Elli will let it go until we can get her home and settled before the interrogation begins.

"I think it's probably best if we cover the basics here, for everyone's sake. That way Elli can ask all the questions her little heart desires."

I glance over at Elli and the man standing with her, looking sheepish at Elli's onslaught of accusations, but also very determined.

I know that look; I've seen that willpower in Raven the very first night I met her and every day since.

This really is her father. She looks so much like him, apart from the olive tone of his skin and the paleness of hers. I can tell he's aged a lot in the last twenty-five years, but he's definitely the man who was in the photo I found earlier. He runs his hands through his hair and I see the Celtic knot tattoo on his forearm.

He was the one in the car that day.

It's time for some answers.

"Elli, maybe let him breathe for a second so you can get the full story," Raven says, sounding exasperated.

"Sure, but he needs to start talking, because we need to get everything out on the table before the brigade shows up with their own questions," Elli replies.

Raven's father walks back toward the living room and gestures for us to have a seat. "I'll answer all your questions, but she's right, we need to hurry."

I sit down on the couch, tucking Raven into my side and rubbing my thumb across the back of her hand in what I hope is a comforting manner.

She gives me a small smile like she knows what I'm thinking, and again I'm taken aback by how in tune we are.

"Okay, first things first, why the fuck did you kidnap Raven?" Elli is brash and straight to the point, and for once in the short time I've known her, I appreciate it.

"I didn't kidnap her, or at least I didn't intend to." He's rubbing the back of his neck in what seems to be a nervous tick as he proceeds. "As I'm sure you know, I'm Raven's father, Robert Cole Jackson. I frequently come and sit outside of the bookstore to see how she's doing." His eyes shift to Raven almost guiltily, but she nods in understanding, encouraging him to go on. He tells us what transpired in the last eight hours and I feel Raven nodding beside me at certain parts.

I have a thousand questions, but I let the information sink in. Raven is safe and unharmed, and she's got answers about her dad now that I'm not sure she wanted.

"Go ahead, Elli." Raven sighs, and motions toward her friend who is basically holding her mouth closed to keep from bursting at the seams.

"I just…I have so many questions. And as much as I want to be upset with how you handled it, you saved Raven from that man and that's the most important thing. But who are you? Why did you stay away? Do you not think it's creepy to sit outside of your daughter's bookstore and watch her?"

"Elli." Raven's tone is a warning and to be honest, it even scares me a little.

"All right! All right. If you're cool with it that's all that matters. We'll work on daddy issues later because someone tried to *kidnap* you!" Elli's voice raises an octave with each word, like it's just now hitting her how scary this all actually is. "You can't go back to the bookstore! You can't. They know you work there, they probably know you live there. You're staying with me."

"Because that's safer?" I ask, regretting the words as soon as they're out of my mouth but it's too late.

Three heads swivel to me at once.

Raven's eyes are hard and slightly annoyed, Elli looks like she could take my head off but I can see she realizes I'm right, and Raven's dad—again—looks determined.

He turns his eyes to Raven. "You need to stay here."

"No. I'm not going to run. I'm not staying anywhere else. I'm going back to the bookstore and that's that," Raven states.

"Raven, I really feel like—"

I feel Raven tense up beside me as her father protests, and I'm not sure how I know, but I know she's about to explode. No sooner has the thought entered my mind when she starts in on him.

"You've got to be kidding me. You haven't been in my life for twenty-five years. Why do you think you have a say now? I appreciate you *saving* me, I really do. It's been nice

157

to have this little catch-up party and finally know who my father is and all that jazz, but I'm grown. I haven't had a parent in over twenty years, because not only did you leave me, you left me with a crackhead. But you know, I've actually done pretty well for myself, raising myself and making my own decisions. And while I appreciate the help, it's not necessary. So with all due respect, *sir,* I'm the only one who gets to make decisions about my life."

Thirty-Seven

Raven

The words are out of my mouth before I realize it and I wish I could say I regret them, but I don't.

I am thankful that my "father" saved me from the rapist/kidnapper/whatever the hell is going on there. I am glad that he brought me here to his home to explain things to me. I had given up on getting answers for the questions I did have about him. I'd grown used to thinking of myself as not having any parents, even though I knew they were probably both out there somewhere.

Being on my own never bothered me, and honestly, it's been less messy that way.

Over the last week I'd decided to let Emmett in, now my dad is barging in, and it's just too much for me.

I see the hurt flash across my father's eyes before he instantly corrects his features to show a steel and stormy resolve.

Looks like I got that from him as well.

"I understand." He gets up and walks into the kitchen, asking if anyone wants something to drink, and there's another knock at the door.

"Showtime," Emmett mutters under his breath and I sigh.

Time to repeat the story for a third time.

An hour later all the details are hashed out again. I'm obviously not pressing charges against my dad for "kidnapping" me, so once we've told the responding officers what occurred in the last ten hours, they have a med tech check me over to make sure I'm okay and say I'm free to go, but that they'll be in contact and I should plan a trip down to the station tomorrow to try to give more details about my attacker and would-be kidnapper.

Despite my earlier outburst, I'm not quite ready to leave my father's house, so I tell them I'll ride back with Elli and Detective Fisher and plan to come in tomorrow afternoon.

Emmett walks them out—I'm sure to talk about the case without raising suspicion about his involvement with me.

Elli seems to have crashed from the adrenaline rush and she's snoring softly on the couch.

My dad is sitting at the kitchen bar, staring into his coffee cup.

I study his hands cupping the mug. I've always heard you can tell a lot about a man from his hands. They're tan, partly from his olive skin tone, but I'm sure he sees a lot of sun here on the beach. They're probably double the size of mine, with long skinny fingers. They're solid hands. The kind that are hard to imagine cradling a small child, even harder to imagine steadying a wobbling toddler. Hands that give a firm handshake. Hands that, in another life, would've escorted me down the aisle on my wedding day.

I think over what I've learned in the last few hours. Either choice in his decision would have left someone without a father.

And I have brothers? Where is his current wife?

I look around but I don't see any family photos on the walls, just art. There are so many answers that I still need, but I'm exhausted.

"You're welcome to stay the night. There's no point in driving back so late when I have two extra guest rooms." His voice startles me out of my musing and I nod.

I must look as tired as I feel. I don't want Emmett driving back at this hour anyway, and Elli is already snoozing away.

"Okay, thank you. I'll wake Elli and head upstairs. Could you let Emmett know when he comes in?"

He nods and I head over to the couch to rouse Elli.

"Hey, sleepyhead. Come on, we're going upstairs," I tell her.

She peeps an eye open at me and sits up slowly, trying to remember where she is.

"I know, this is weird. We're going to stay here tonight and head back in the morning. Up you go, come on." I get her up and lead her to the room beside the one I woke up in earlier, careful not to bump her side where her ribs are injured.

I flip on the light and reveal a room almost opposite to mine. The walls are painted a soft orange color, and the furniture is gray wicker. There's a huge canvas over the bed with the sun setting across the water and the bedding is shades of bright red, orange, and yellow.

It's interesting that my dad didn't choose this room for me, and instead put me in the calm gray and pale blue room beside it. This one is much better suited for Elli's personality. I tuck her into bed like a child and she grabs my hand before I leave.

"I'm so glad you're okay, Rave. We'll figure all of this out, I promise," she says on a yawn, and she's asleep again before I can reply.

Brushing her hair out of her face, I notice that her bruises have turned a dull green. I ease out of her room and pad down the hallway to what I'm assuming is the bathroom, pretty sure the master bedroom is on the main level. I let out a sigh of relief when I find that I'm correct and close the door, leaning against the back of it for a minute.

I take a deep breath and turn to look in the mirror. It's easier to see my father's features in my face now. There are even matching dark circles under my eyes.

What are we going to do now, Raven Jackson?

Thirty-Eight

Emmett

I meant to quickly walk the officers out—Carolina Beach department had also shown up, seeing as we were in their jurisdiction—but it took longer than I expected. When we were out of Raven's earshot, we had to go over new case details.

We've had the tech department on the hunt for any traffic cameras that recorded Brent driving to or away from Poe's, But Raven only has one security camera in the bookstore, and of course it's pointed toward the cash register. I'm kicking myself for not having entry and exit cameras installed after the letter mysteriously showed up, but everything else seemed more pressing at the time. I make a mental note to have some installed the moment I have a chance.

The EMT took a blood sample from Raven to see if we could determine what type of sedative the attacker gave her, but it'll be days before the results come back. Whoever's behind this is getting reckless, and although that scares me to no end, hopefully he's also getting sloppy so we can catch him.

By the time I get back inside, the downstairs lights are out and Robert is the only one awake. I find him sitting at the kitchen bar.

"The girls went on to bed. Raven decided it would be better to stay here for the night and leave in the morning." Before I can say anything, he adds, "I know I've messed up with her. I've missed so much of her life."

I look longingly at the stairs, ready to snuggle my girl and sleep off the hellish day we've had but instead I take the seat beside him. "Honestly, I haven't been dating Raven long, I don't even know if she'd call it dating, but regardless I feel like I know her well enough to know that she needs time to process all of this right now. She's not an emotional person, and from what I've seen she likes her space and alone time. I think she realizes that you had a tough decision to make. I'd just give her some time and maybe when she's ready you two can sit down and talk everything out. I don't know what the future will look like for the both of you, but I do think Raven will be fair and give you a fighting chance."

He turns to look me directly in the eyes. "And what about your future?"

"What do you mean?"

"With Raven," he clarifies.

"I'm not sure. I know what I want, and I *think* I know what she wants. But she's got to let herself trust me and I think that may take time. I'm willing to wait, though. She'd be worth waiting for forever."

A little smirk appears at the corner of his mouth and I think I see a glimmer of approval in his eyes. "She sounds just like her mother," he starts to say, and then shakes his head. "I'd probably do well to keep that to myself."

I smile back at him and say, "I doubt it would do you any favors to compare the two in any capacity. I'm sure the woman you knew and the woman she knew are two very different people."

"Must be, because the woman I knew would never have let her daughter not be in her life."

I think about what Raven has shared with me about her mother and the similarities between her and my father and shrug. "Drugs will do that to you. I'm going to head upstairs. Thank you, for letting us stay the night, and for saving Raven today."

"I'd do anything for her," he states, and resumes staring at his coffee cup.

When I glance back at him from the top of the stairs, that's what he's still doing. If I were a betting man I'd put my money on him staying that way all night.

It can't be easy to meet the daughter you've watched from afar for twenty-five years on the same day she almost gets kidnapped by a rapist, and then find out that the love of your life has turned into a drug addict and abandoned the daughter you thought was well taken care of.

I send up a silent wish that Raven will give him a shot when all of this is over.

Thirty-Nine

Raven

I had left the bedroom door cracked when I got into bed, so I heard the majority of Emmett's conversation with my dad.

My heart is so full, and my brain is so confused.

I know Emmett cares about me, and I know I care about him. Despite my earlier resolve to take things slow with him, I can feel myself falling fast and I know I need to rein it in. But when I heard him defending my actions and advising my dad not to compare me to my mother...

It's like he understands my soul, and I've never felt that way before. Part of me thinks Emmett Fisher could be my safe place, my soulmate. The other—*larger?*—part of me knows how foolish that sounds.

I hear him walk up to the door and smile at how quiet he's trying to be. I let him think I'm asleep for a few more minutes just so I can watch him.

He takes off his jacket, then his shoes and socks, and then his shirt. I feel my stomach flip at the sight of his bare chest, thankful for the small lamp in the corner throwing a little light across the hard planes of his chest and stomach.

When he shuffles out of his pants, my heart rate speeds up. I'm thankful he closed the bedroom door, because if I could hear their conversation downstairs there's no doubt my father would be able to hear what's about to go down in this room.

He climbs into bed beside me, turning toward me, sliding his arm under my pillow and leaning forward to kiss my forehead.

I open my eyes and grin at him.

"Why aren't you asleep?" he asks with a smile, wrapping his other arm around me and pulling me to his chest.

"I was waiting for you." I know he's exhausted and I'm not sure if he's up for what I have in mind, but I decide to test the waters anyway.

"Oh yeah?"

He buries his face into my hair and I nod, sliding my hand down his chest to the waistband of his boxers, letting him know my intentions.

"Are you sure?" he asks. "I know you're exhausted—"

"Haven't we had this talk before? I'll decide when I'm exhausted, and right now I need you inside of me. So if you're too tired, tell me now and I'll let you have your sleep. If not, stop talking."

I feel him instantly go rock-hard, so I dip my hand into his boxers and wait for his reply.

"You're going to kill me, woman."

I take that as the invite I'd been waiting for and wrap my hand around his cock, marveling at the hardness and length. We groan at the same time, and he thrusts his hips up involuntarily.

"Yes, this is exactly what I need," I whisper into his ear, nibbling and sucking on his ear lobe.

"Raven, get undressed. Now, please." He's trying to sound like he's in charge but we both know he's not.

I oblige and let go of him to do so, instantly regretting the loss of contact.

He tosses his boxers across the room and he's hovering over me before I can even blink. "I don't have a condom. I didn't think to grab—"

"I'm on the pill. It's fine, I trust you."

"Are you sure? We can—"

"Emmett!"

"Yes ma'am." And with that he thrusts into me in one fluid movement, almost making me scream with relief and pleasure.

I let out a hiss, trying to keep quiet.

"Fuck, Raven."

I can hear the strain in his voice and I grin. "You feel so good, Emmett."

"Holy shit."

"I want to ride you."

He pushes his forehead against mine, eyes shut tight and trying to control his breathing. He slides out of me and rolls over, grabbing my hips as he goes and settling me on top of him.

I align us and start to slide down onto his cock as slowly as I can manage.

"Goddamn you really *are* going to kill me." He tries bucking his hips up but I lift out of reach and give him another grin.

"Stop moving or it'll be slower," I tease.

He groans but gives in and I continue my downward descent. When he's finally all the way inside of me, I start grinding against him, lifting up and sliding down as I go.

"Raven, I seriously can't fucking last with you like this. You're so fucking beautiful." He palms my breasts and tweaks my nipples as I roll my hips.

I let out a moan as he fills me again and I increase my pace, reaching down to steady myself on his chest. "I love the way you feel inside of me. I'm not sure why we didn't do this bare sooner." I slide up and then slam back down onto him.

"Raven!" He yelps and I feel his hips start to buck as he presses his thumb into my clit.

That's all it takes and I'm flying over the edge, splintering into a million pieces on top of him while I feel him explode inside of me.

We stay like that for a few minutes, catching our breath and letting our heart rates slow.

"Holy shit," he says on an exhale.

"I know." I smirk. "You've said that." I lean over him to kiss him, his length still inside of me.

He puts his hand on the back of my head, pulling me closer and making me feel like he can't get enough of me.

I slide off of him and slink to the door, grabbing his shirt to slide over my head before I slip down the hallway to clean up. Elli comes out of the bathroom and I grin at her sheepishly.

"I really hope we didn't wake you," I say.

She's still half asleep and I think I hear her mumble a playful insult as she passes and stumbles into her room.

I smile and hustle to get back in bed with my guy.

Forty

Emmett

Holy shit.

I know, I've said and thought that about seven times in the last twenty minutes, but really.

...Holy shit.

I clean up with some tissues beside the bed, snag my boxers from across the room, and get back into bed to wait for her.

I'm exhausted, satiated, and beyond relieved to have her in bed with me again tonight. Just a few hours ago I wasn't sure what the next twenty-four hours would hold. The thought that I could've lost her today makes me want to puke. I know she's told me she doesn't want a relationship over and over, but I have to let her know how important she is to me—even if it falls on deaf ears.

I hear her tiptoeing back into the room and I pull the covers back for her. She settles in, letting out a content sigh as I rub circles on her lower back, and I love that she's wearing my shirt.

"I need to talk to you about something," I say.

She goes stiff, and I rush to finish my thought before she bolts.

"It's nothing bad. I just…today scared the shit out of me, gorgeous."

She nods against my chest, and I can feel her start to relax again.

"I know that this, whatever this is, is not something you were looking for," I start. "I can respect that. I also know this is the sixth night in a row that we've been in the same bed at the end of the day, and I know that has to mean something to you, too."

She nods again, not giving me a word, and I smirk as I go for the gut.

"I think I'm falling for you, Raven, and I know that scares you. Hell, it scares me. I just need you to know. I never want to feel the way I felt this evening again. I'm not expecting you to feel the same right now, and you don't even need to say anything. I just need you to know." I hold my breath and brace myself, expecting her to roll over to put her back to me, but she doesn't.

"Okay," she says.

Okay? That's all?

I'll take it.

I kiss her forehead and snuggle her closer to my side, rubbing her hair and listening to her breathing even out as she falls asleep.

The next morning comes and goes, as none of us had any alarms set. I think we were all too exhausted to care about waking up early to get back to town.

It's after ten when I finally decide to wake the sleeping beauty next to me, kissing her softly on the lips and then with more pressure until I feel her stir underneath me.

"Morning." I nudge her with my face as her eyes sleepily open.

She shakes her head and tries to roll over and I chuckle.

"I know, gorgeous. It's after ten, though, and I didn't know if you had anyone to cover the bookstore."

Nevermore

"Shit," she grumbles and rolls off the bed, searching the dresser across the room for her phone and bringing it to her ear. "Missy? Hey, yeah, I'm fine. I know. I'm sorry. I know everyone was worried sick but I'm okay. Could you have Jason run down to the store and make sure there are no stragglers waiting out front? And maybe put a note on the door saying we'll open at noon? I should be there in about an hour. Thank you so much, you guys are life-savers."

She hangs up the phone and winks at me, heading to wake Elli, I assume, so we can get on the road.

Forty-One

Raven

We're almost back to the store when Elli starts to hyperventilate. She's in the backseat and I'm riding shotgun when I hear her start to wheeze.

"Pull over," I whisper under my breath to Emmett.

He pulls over onto the shoulder of the highway and I jump in the backseat with her. Her eyes are frantic and her chest is heaving.

"Okay, E, I've got you. Where's your head right now?" I slide my arm around her shoulders and pull her to me, cradling her head against my chest. She knows I'm a touch-me-not but I know this is what she needs right now. I'm sure she'll rib me about it later.

"I just…how can we…you can't go back there…he almost *kidnapped* you, Raven!"

"I know, I know. And I know this is also about what he did to you. It's okay to be upset, Elli. It's okay to be scared." I catch Emmett's eyes in the rearview mirror and give him a slight head nod to let him know I think I can calm her down.

I knew this was coming sooner or later, and I think I'm prepared enough, although she's only had one other panic attack in front of me before. Elli doesn't crack easily.

"Let's try to breathe through it," I tell her. I know if I can get her grounded before she spirals too hard, we can talk it out. "Tell me three things you can physically feel right now. Come on, I'll help you. Can you feel the seat against your back?"

She nods against my chest.

"Okay great, what else?"

"I can feel your hair in my face," she says, and I hold back a chuckle and wait for her to continue. "And I can feel this seatbelt cutting into my hip."

All rainbows and sunshine as usual.

I move to unclick her belt and a sob escapes her.

"All right, all right," I soothe as I pull my hair over my shoulder. "My hair is out of your face and the belt is off. Tell me three things you can smell."

"This...is...so...dumb." Her breathing picks up again between her words and she's clutching her hair in her fist.

"I know, but humor your counselor best friend, please?"

She nods and takes a deep breath. "Your hair smells like apples. I can smell Emmett's vanilla air freshener, and I'm not digging it to be honest." Again, I fight a chuckle, then she adds, "I can smell the leather from the seat."

"Okay, that's good. What are three things you can hear?"

"Me, blubbering like an idiot." Her sobs are calmer as she tries to gather herself. "I can hear the cars going by on the highway. And I can hear your heartbeat, which is a lot slower than mine. You really are good at this shit, huh?" She finishes on a deep shuddering breath.

"Yeah, I'm a badass. Do we need to keep going or are you back to your badass self, too?"

"I think I'm okay." She picks her head up off of my chest and looks me in the eyes, trying to assure both of us. The steely resolve is back in her baby blues and I feel myself relax a little.

"You want to talk about it?"

"Nope. I just need to make a phone call to my security company. I'm going to double the team and send half to stay with you if you're determined to stay in that bookstore," she says.

I open my mouth to argue but catch Emmett's eye again in the mirror and see him shaking his head, urging me not to and just let her do this. I know they're right. It'll calm all of our nerves, even though the thought of having a security detail twenty-four/seven makes me want to have a panic attack of my own. "Fine, E. Just until we figure out who's behind this. Are you okay to get back on the road?"

"Yeah, let's go," she says, and I keep my arm around her, deciding to stay in the back with her for the remainder of the ride.

When we pull up to the bookstore, I'm a little surprised to see that everything looks normal.

There's no crime scene tape, no glass or discarded car parts on the street out front. I don't know what I was expecting, but I'm relieved to find that my baby is fine.

Emmett pulls around back and I take my keys out so we can enter through the rear entrance. Reggie is here, saving my ass and running the show like usual.

"Reg?" I brace myself, knowing he's either going to cry or scream at me.

I see a flurry of gray but before I can register what's happening, he's launched himself at me and we're on the ground.

"Oh! *Ohhh*! You! I'm so fucking mad at you, Raven Jackson!" he says.

A sound escapes me but he's squeezing me so hard that I can't form actual words.

"I'm so happy you're all right but you scared the ever-living shit out of me and I'm *furious,* Raven, do you hear me? Furious!"

He finally releases me when Emmett clears his throat, whom I steal a glance up at to see he's barely restraining himself from pulling Reggie off of me.

I give him a small smile to reassure him that I'm fine. We clamber to our feet and Reggie wraps me in a hug again.

"Really, I was so scared, Rave," Reggie says in a much quieter voice, looking like a little boy instead of the twenty-three-year-old man he is.

"I know, I'm so sorry. I don't know what I was thinking but I promise to never do that to you again."

He nods and finally releases me. "Todd may also kill you."

"I figured. I owe you both another vacation. How about a spa day?" I offer.

He hooks his arm over my shoulder and shakes his head, then we walk to the front of the store, which I'm relieved to find empty.

"Everything been okay so far today?" I ask him.

"Yeah, it's been slow."

I nod and turn to Elli. "Do you want Emmett to take you home?"

"Nah, I drove here. I'll be fine."

"Uh, I actually need to go by the station and file my report. Why don't I just follow you home before I swing by the station?" Emmett meets my eyes over her head and I hope he can tell how thankful I am for his suggestion.

I think she's calmed down enough, but I don't want her having a breakdown on the ten-minute drive to her place with no one there to help her.

"All right, sounds good," she concedes, and I know her pride is bucking, but I'm sure she knows we're just concerned for her.

"Reggie, do you mind if I head upstairs and jump in the bath for a few? I just need to recharge and process some of this," I say to him.

"Of course not. I'll hold down the fort."

I owe him so much.

I head upstairs, calling the boujie spa uptown that I know he loves, and I book him and Todd the works for tomorrow.

Wrenn Montgomery

Forty-Two

Emmett

I follow Elliott home and make sure she's safely in her building before stopping by my apartment to change into new clothes and make myself look presentable.

There's a stack of mail at my door—probably because I haven't checked all week and the mail lady couldn't fit any more in my mailbox.

I've got to get better at this.

I bend down and scoop them up before unlocking the door. Walking into the kitchen, I toss the mail on the counter and sort through it, separating the bills from everything else. At the bottom of the pile are three letters from my dad. I usually don't write him back, but he sends them anyway, wanting to know how Everette and Emerson are doing, wanting to know how my injury is healing, wanting to know what I've been up to, asking me to come visit. It's hard, knowing your old man couldn't handle the heartbreak of losing the love of his life and turned to drugs to help himself cope.

When I was younger it just infuriated me, knowing that the boys and I weren't enough for him to keep his head on straight. But the older I get, the more I understand how deeply he felt her loss and how hard it must've been for a father with three young boys to raise on his own. And now that I've met Raven, it's even easier to understand.

Maybe I should write him back more often.

I put that thought away for another day.

I shower and dress quickly, anxious to get this over with and get back to her. I'm sure that the captain has received word that I stayed with Raven last night. I'm not going to be able to brush that off as extra investigating. I just hope he doesn't throw me off the case. Checking myself over in the mirror, I snag my badge and weapon and head out.

The quick walk to the station allows me to collect my thoughts and try to figure out what I'm going to say to my boss. I think honesty is the best policy, and if it gets me kicked off the case then maybe I'll take a few personal days and spend some time with Raven to make sure if someone comes for her again, I'll be there to protect her and nail them.

As I walk down the sidewalk and approach the station, taking in the scene around me, I see a man playing a banjo out in the square with an open suitcase at his feet. I can smell the scent of sweets and goodies drifting out of the bakery I pass. Everyone smiles, waves, or tips their hat as I walk by.

Moving down south was the right decision for me. I've never felt more at home than I do here. Back in Delaware, most of my memories are bad ones. I barely remember my mom, and it's hard to find a handful of good memories with my father.

Most consist of taking care of the boys and trying to keep them and myself out of trouble. When I think on it, it's a damn miracle we all got out alive and not addicted to one vice or another. Although it may say something about the three of us that we all jumped into infantry as soon as we turned eighteen just to escape the place we grew up.

I'm damn proud of my brothers, though—and even myself—for getting the hell out of there. I landed on my feet here in North Carolina after almost dying for my country. I found the job I believe I was meant to do all along, in the place I was meant to do it.

I just hope the girl that I think I'm meant to be with doesn't keep shutting me out.

Forty-Three

Raven

An hour later, I'm done with my bath and ready to face the world again. I've processed all there is to process.

I get dressed and make my way downstairs.

Reggie is behind my desk, looking much more relaxed, and he gives me a smile as I approach. "You look better."

"I was thinking the same about you." I lean against the corner of the desk and look over his shoulder at the computer screen. He's adding up receipts from the week, something I usually handle.

"You want to take over?" He sounds bored out of his mind, and I stifle a giggle.

I love the numbers; he doesn't.

"Yes, but I promised the officers from last night that I'd go into the station today to finish giving my statement. I shouldn't be long. Are you okay here?"

"Yes, Mother. I'm fine."

I chuckle and grab my jacket from the coat tree behind him. Sliding it on, I catch Emmett's scent and take a deep breath in.

"You're fucked," he says.

"Excuse me?"

"You're in love with him."

"Reggie," I say, with warning in my tone.

"You know it, I know it, I think he knows it."

"He told me he was falling for me last night," I admit.

"And you said?"

"I said okay, which, you know, was good for me. I didn't bolt."

"And that's a freaking miracle in itself, *but*...you need to let him know how you feel, Rave. You can do it."

I nod and start to back away, grinning. He knows I'm avoiding this like the plague, but he loves me enough to let it go. "I'll hurry back, I promise."

"Perfect. Oh, and your new friends are here."

"What new fr—"

My sentence trails off as I see who he's referring to. There's an entourage of bodyguards waiting for me. Okay, there's two of them, but still.

"Fuck me," I mutter.

I hear Reggie laughing as I make my way over to them.

I sit in a large and surprisingly comfortable desk chair in the lower level of the police station. The fact that Emmett is somewhere in this building soothes me, but I'm nervous nonetheless. I know I don't have a reason to be, but I'm just ready to get this over with.

My new bodyguards are waiting in the lobby behind me. I guess they assume I'm safe enough here.

"Thanks for coming in, Miss Jackson." The woman behind the desk has a round, kind face. Rosy cheeks, tortoise shell glasses, flowery top with hot pink pants. She reminds me of a vice principal, nice but firm.

For the next forty-five minutes we go over what happened again.

"If you could just read back over your statement, make sure it's all true, and then sign here at the bottom to verify that it's correct." She slides a pen over to me and I scan it quickly.

Everything looks good, so I sign it and she stands, then I follow suit.

"I'm going to lead you over here to our sketch artist, if you're okay with that?"

"Sure," I say.

I follow her across the lobby area to another office and wait as she knocks. I hear a gruff, "Come in," and she opens the door for me. The smell of cigars hits me in the face.

Behind the desk there's a small middle-aged man. He's wearing khaki pants, a blue checkered button-up, and his hair is greasy, like he hasn't washed it in a few days. "I'm Mike."

"Raven." I shake his outstretched hand.

"Nice to meet you, Raven."

The secretary promises to come back to get me when I'm finished, then leaves us in his office.

"I know this is a rough time for you, darlin'. I hate that we have to rehash it like this, but we gotta make sure we get the right guy, you know? Let's start simple. Can you tell me what color his hair is?"

I close my eyes, and for the next fifteen minutes I try my best to visualize the man who tried to kidnap me. I give Mike all I can, right down to the way the guy's two front teeth were turned slightly to the left.

When we're finished, he sets his tablet down and tells me I've done a great job. "I think we've got something, I really do. We'll compare this to the surveillance video from the hotel and the sketch from the other victim and see if it's a match."

I stare at him blankly.

Hotel? What hotel?

We have surveillance video of him?

Before I can ask, the secretary—I want to say her name was Susan—returns.

Maybe-Susan leads me back to the main lobby, promising to call me if they need anything else from me.

As I turn to leave, I spot a familiar silhouette on the balcony above me.

Emmett.

Forty-Four

Emmett

I hear Raven's voice float up to me from the main level of the station and walk over to the balcony to catch a glimpse of her.

Right as my eyes land on her, she lifts hers to meet mine, like she just knew I'd be there. I smile at her, and hold my finger up, indicating I'll be right down.

But when I reach the bottom of the stairs, she's gone.

I jog through the lobby and out the front door, looking down the sidewalk for her. I spot her a few yards down. Two men are walking close to her in the same uniforms as the guards at Elli's house.

"Raven!"

She spins slowly and waits for me to catch up, but I sense her reluctance.

"What's wrong?" I ask her.

She shrugs, fiddling with the zipper on her coat and looking anywhere but at me. "I don't know, I just…I don't know. Why didn't you tell me about the hotel footage?"

My head tilts a little to the side. "I wasn't trying to keep it from you. We found out right before Reggie called me to say you had been taken. We're pretty sure he left the hotel and went straight to the bookstore to grab you, knowing we were on to him. I was planning on talking to you about it and what we found there, but I just haven't really had a chance and I got sidetracked by everything else that happened."

She seems to contemplate this for a second then looks up at me, and I can see her expression has lifted a little, but she's skeptical. "All right."

I know the conversation isn't over yet, but I change the subject and decide to revisit it later. "How did everything go at the station?"

"Fine, I think. I gave a description to the sketch artist. He said they'd compare it to the hotel footage. I need to get back to the store. Can we talk about it later?" She's looking over my shoulder while she talks, not making eye contact with me.

Body language is something that I've been trained to pick up on, and hers is screaming that she doesn't want to be here with me right now.

"Yeah, okay. I'll call you when I get off?" I try.

She gives me a small smile and backs away. Her bodyguards close in around her and I can only see the curtain of black hair swinging as she walks away.

I blow out a breath and walk back to the station, unsure of what just happened.

Forty-Five

Raven

The drive back to my store is quiet, but a little tense. I have one of the bodyguards in the car with me; his name is Phil. The other is following behind us in another vehicle. Phil doesn't speak unless spoken to, and it's annoying the shit out of me.

"You can talk, you know," I state.

"Yes, ma'am." I see the start of a smile at the corner of his mouth and let it rest.

I'm taking my annoyance out on him and it's not fair. Even though I know he listened carefully to my exchange with Emmett and it bothers me.

He's just doing his job.

I repeat this to myself over and over.

Plus, he let me drive, which impressed me.

"All right, Phil," I say to him, breaking the silence yet again as I look over at him, "if you're going to be hanging around for a few days, can we at least get to know each other a little?"

He chuckles and asks, "What would you like to know, Miss Jackson?"

"Please just call me Raven."

"Okay, Miss Raven."

I roll my eyes and hold back a groan. *He's just doing his job.* "Are you married, Phil?"

"Yes ma'am."

"How long?"

"Twenty years this May."

"Wow. So you know a lot about…relationships and stuff." *Why am I so awkward?*

He chuckles again, his voice gruff and rusty. "Yep."

"Well, that's great. I'm happy for you."

"Excuse me for being forward here, Miss Raven, but is there something else you're trying to ask me?"

Oh, so he's intuitive. Brains and brawn.

I'm busted and I feel my face heating up. "I just…you heard all of that back there, right?"

"Yes, ma'am."

"And what did you think?"

"Do you want my honest opinion?" he asks me.

I look over and hold his gaze for a second, not entirely sure if I do or not. I finally decide to take a chance and say, "Yes, please."

"I don't think you trust anyone. You don't like the silence in this car because you don't trust me. You're trying to fill it with small talk to keep yourself from feeling anxious. You don't trust that fellow either, but I think you want to. I don't think he kept anything from you. I think you're looking for something to be mad about so you have a reason not to trust him."

Damn.

"Oh."

"I apologize, if that was—"

"No, no, don't apologize. You're right." I take a deep breath, and for some reason, I begin to spill my guts to this bodyguard I just met today. "I like him. And I promised myself I'd give him a chance, but I do think I'm trying to sabotage it. I need to cool it a little."

He just nods and continues looking around us, like he's constantly looking for threats, and as we pull up to the store I whisper a small thank you, to which he shrugs and says, "Anytime, Miss Raven."

A few hours pass and I'm waiting for Emmett to call while manning the front desk.

We're not super busy today, but we've had a steady flow and it's been nice to focus on work for a little while. Although the three large men wandering around the shop and standing by the entrances are a little distracting, I do feel safer with them here. Reggie is still here, too. He's in the back, unpacking T-shirts for the inventory room.

I decide to text Emmett.

Me: Hey, I'm sorry about earlier.

I see the dots of him typing his response and I hold my breath. I suck at apologizing, but it's easier over text and I hope he doesn't think I'm being insincere. My phone dings.

Emmett: Don't be sorry. I'll tell you all about it tonight. I promise.

I instantly feel better.

Of course he'd accept my apology this easily.

He's a saint.

Me: Can't wait.

I put my phone down and smile to myself, knowing I really need to just chill out.

Emmett hasn't given me any reason not to trust him, and yet I'm looking for one at every turn.

The door opens to the shop and the little bell over it dings. Out of habit, I look up.

Lacey is walking toward me, with a grin on her face that I can't quite place.

Wrenn Montgomery

Forty-Six

Emmett

After reading Raven's text, I relax a little. Until I hear the captain say my name.

Shit.

"Yes, sir?"

"Come see me in my office when you finish up."

I stand, close my laptop, and follow him back to his office since my work for the day is already finished. Once I close the door behind me, I sit down in the same old rickety chair that I sat in last week, and mentally prepare myself for this chat.

"I don't like you on this case, son."

I open my mouth to respond and he cuts me off.

"Let me finish. I don't like you on this case because I know you're too close to it." I've seen you with her. However, at this point, I think taking you off of the case would do more damage than leaving you on it. I understand someone has hired security for her, correct?"

"Yes, sir."

"Perfect. So her safety is no longer your concern, correct?"

"To be honest sir, her safety will always be my concern. But yes, there is additional help in that area now," I tell him.

"Understood. So with her safety squared away, you can focus solely on the case, and not just on her. I want you on it, Fisher. You and Tropp. You have the info at your hands, you have her at your hands, you can get inside information. Don't come into the station unless it's pertinent or you have a lead to work. Don't worry about being here. Stay by her side. Be there for any phone calls or visitors she gets. Go through her past with her. Do what you gotta do to get this solved. We've got one high-profile female attorney who was attacked, and a near-miss kidnapping that happened right under our noses. I want this finished. Let's close this case and get him and whoever hired him. Tell me your theories and we'll go from there."

"Thank you, sir." I tell him what we've got so far, most of which he already knows, before I stand to leave and he stands with me, shaking my hand and dismissing me with a nod toward the door.

That was not what I was expecting, not in the least bit. But I thank my lucky stars and head over to Raven's to tell her what I know.

Forty-Seven

Raven

"Raven!"

Lacey is walking toward me, looking like she came straight from a music festival, and I guess she did. There's glitter all over her body. Her denim shorts are just barely covering her ass, and she has ripped brown tights underneath them. There's some sort of star painted on her cheek, and her red hair hosts a rainbow of ribbons. She's wearing suspenders over a tight cropped tank top.

The looks she must have gotten walking down Main Street in this small town make me want to smirk, but instead I ask, "How was your trip?"

"Oh my gosh, it was amazing. The most spiritual experience of my life. I mean, I really had a breakthrough!"

Reggie must've heard her, as he comes out of the storage room to conveniently start stocking the front shelves. Phil is hovering somewhere behind me, and Mark is somewhere outside of the building.

"That's wonderful, Lacey." I shuffle through the top drawer, looking for her check.

"Yeah, I mean, there's been so much negativity lately…around you, this store, my life. I'm just so glad that it's finally over. I mean, it's not, but it is, you know?" She's rattling on, the seventy billion bracelets on her arm jingling as she waves her arms around talking about the festival and all the 'experiences' she had there.

I'm half-listening, still trying to find her check.

"What do you mean, Lacey?" Reggie pipes up and shoots me a look.

I finally find the check, which I could've sworn was right on top but is now buried under several receipt books. I pull it out and look up at them, something strange crossing Lacey's face.

"What negativity has been around Raven and this store?" he asks her.

"It's really none of your concern, Reggie."

Reggie chuckles and my hackles start to rise.

"Lacey, here's your check. I think you'd better go now," I say.

"No, wait." Reggie shoots me another look. "What negative things have been happening? I'd love to know."

"Uh," Lacey stammers, and Reggie crosses his arms, eyebrows creeping up to his hairline. "Well, I just heard that you were attacked, Raven. But you look really good!"

"You heard Raven was attacked?" he presses.

"Yeah, and in the hospital. How scary!" she says.

"And where did you hear that, Lacey?" Reggie is like a dog with a bone, and he's not letting this go.

"Oh, just around. And what a pity! But honestly, Raven, you can't even tell!"

I've had enough. I'm not sure what's going on here but I'm ready for her to leave. "I actually wasn't attacked, per se, and I'm fine. Thank you for coming by and saving me a stamp." I hand her the check and she takes it, a look of confusion on her face.

"Oh, well, of course. Have a great night!" Her voice elevates at the end of her sentence.

Phil is suddenly right behind me as Lacey turns and almost runs out of the store, pulling her phone out as she runs. It's to her ear before she's out of my sight.

"What in the actual fuck was that?" I ask, looking at Reggie.

"I don't know, but how did she know any of that? None of it has been on the news…"

He's right, because Elli threatened to sue any media outlet that ran a story on her and she has such good connections with them that they didn't want to piss her off.

"I know," I say.

"I think we need to call Emmett," Reggie states.

"Already on it," Phil pipes up from behind me.

My belly is doing flips, and I can feel the bile raising in my throat. "You think…you think she was involved?"

"Why else would she conveniently skip town the week all this happened? She looked surprised to see you here, and she thought you had been attacked. Something isn't right," Reggie says.

I nod, and suddenly it makes too much sense.

"Emmett is on his way," Phil says, and Mark appears a few seconds later.

"I'm going to close up and head upstairs," I tell them. "Do you guys have to come up with me, or how is this going to work?"

"I'd like you to take this panic button," Phil says, handing me a key fob. "But we'll stay down here."

"You're not going to sleep?" I ask him.

"B Team will relieve us at nine PM. We'll go home and be back at nine AM to switch off with them. But no, they won't be sleeping. They'll continue to case the premises and keep watch."

"Okay, thank you," I say, before heading to the front of the store.

I flip the sign to "Closed" and shut off the outside lights.

When I turn to close the shutters, I see Lacey on her phone, standing across the street, staring right at me.

Forty-Eight

Emmett

Fucking Lacey.

I should've vetted that one. She has to be the one that was feeding information to Brent Smallwood. That file he had, the things he knew...

They had to have come from someone who was close to her and seeing her on a daily basis. Lacey was the perfect mole.

I rush to Raven's store and nod to the bodyguards as I pull up.

Lacey is long gone.

When the security detail had gone to approach her outside, she bolted.

Thank God they're here.

Reggie also waited for me. "She's upstairs," he informs me when I enter the stock room in the back.

"Probably in the bath," we say in unison.

"Can you tell me what Lacey said? I need to take a statement and send it to Tropp," I say.

Phil, the larger of the security guards, comes over to tell me what he heard; and with his and Reggie's recollection of events I have enough to bring her in for questioning.

They sign the statement we write out, and I call Tropp.

She's been in a nearby county trying to track down Raven's mom. I'm not sure how Raven will take this information, but I'm going to tell her about it tonight.

"Tropp."

"Hey, Monica. Anything?" I ask her.

"Yeah, I found her. She's in bad shape but swears she doesn't owe anyone anything and doesn't know a single person who would want to hurt Raven. She's concerned of course, and is wanting to make contact with her. I told her we'd let Raven know and that we'd let her decide how she wanted to proceed."

"All right, good. It's a touchy subject, but I'll bring it up with her tonight." I tell her about the situation with Lacey, and my meeting with the captain.

"I'm going to stay here and discuss everything with Raven. I'll let you know where we get from there. If you find Lacey, please call me. I want to be there for her interview," I tell her.

She agrees and we hang up.

I say goodbye to Reggie and Phil walks him to the door, making sure he gets to Todd's car safely.

Then, I bolt up the stairs to get to Raven.

This is going to be a hard night, but I hope she'll have more trust in me after all the cards are on the table.

I find her in the bath, just like Reggie and I figured. I knock on the big wooden door to the bathroom and she tells me to come in.

Raven in a tub full of bubbles is a sight I hope to never forget.

I take her in for a moment, seeing her and only her, and then slowly the rest of the world comes back into focus. She has a wooden tray laying across the tub in front of her. On the tray is a bottle of wine, a wine glass, a candle…and a plate of bacon.

Of course.

Her pitch-black hair is piled on top of her head in a messy knot, and she's taken her makeup off but left all her jewelry on. She always wears a short chain necklace with a small silver half-moon on it, and about five rings on her fingers. I can see her toes peeping out of the bubbles at the end of the tub, painted a dark burgundy. Her upper left arm is covered in a black and gray floral tattoo, and it fits her perfectly.

She's perfect.

I slump down on the floor beside the tub, and she holds her hand out so I can hold it. I kiss the back of it and she giggles.

"How cliché, Mr. Fisher."

"That's Detective Fisher to you, ma'am."

She giggles again and makes like she's going to splash me.

"I wouldn't," I say. "The bacon might get wet."

"Oooh, good point." She grabs another slice and crunches down on it, then offers it to me.

"What kind of man would I be for taking a woman's bacon?"

"Well, if you recall, you did the first night."

"I do recall." I smirk and she leans her head back against the tub, closing her eyes with a smile on her lips.

"I know we need to talk, but can we just wait a few minutes? I just want to soak in this moment first."

"We can wait as long as you want, gorgeous."

Forty-Nine

Raven

We stay in the bathroom until the water goes cold and the bubbles are gone.

The patience of this man has me falling a little harder, and I curse myself for the butterflies I get when he offers to help me out of the tub, averting his eyes from my body.

"You don't want to look?" I give him a grin and he clears his throat.

"I always want to look."

"So why aren't you?"

"I want to give you your space, follow your lead. Do you want me to look?"

"You've seen me naked every day for the last week, Emmett." I refrain myself from rolling my eyes.

Now he wants to act shy?

"And I'll never take that for granted or assume that's my right," he says.

"Perfect answer. But yes, you can always look."

He turns toward me, standing in front of the tub on my white marble tile. He starts at my toes and slowly makes his way up my body with his eyes.

By the time he's reached my hips, I'm squirming. The scrutiny is almost unbearable. "What?"

"Just soaking it all in," he says, throwing my earlier words back at me, and I swat at him. Before I make contact he grabs my arm and pulls me to him.

"I'm all wet," I protest, scared of ruining his button-up or slacks.

He ignores me and picks me up, carrying me to the bed across my loft. Laying me down so my head rests upon a pillow, he stands back, looking at me again.

I close my eyes, unable to take it. I'm pretty confident in my body, but this feels like I'm baring my soul to this man and he's just taking his sweet time lapping it up.

"Open your eyes, Raven." I reluctantly follow his directions and he adds, "Don't close them again."

"Yes, sir."

Hearing those words seems to change something in him—his back is a little straighter and his eyes get a glassy gaze.

In less than ten seconds he's naked and hovering over me on the bed. "Say that again."

"Sir."

His eyes close slowly, and then he's moving, making damn sure I know just how much he appreciates me as he worships my body for the next hour.

A while later, we're lying in the dark under the covers and he's drawing small circles on my lower back with his fingertips.

"You ready to talk about everything?" he asks me.

I nod against his chest.

"We've got some theories that I want to run by you. Don't hold anything back, I want to know what you think about them. Some of this is going to be a little uncomfortable, and if it becomes too much, we can stop."

"I'll be fine, Emmett," I say to encourage him. Even if this is hard, I'll get through it. I always do.

"Okay. Our list of suspects is small, and the connection with Lacey could technically be with any of them. I'm really suspicious of her, and I feel like she may have had something to do with this. If we can get her into custody and get her to answer our questions, we may be able to unravel all of this. Monica is out looking for her now. She's going to call me if she finds her."

"Tell me what you found at the hotel."

He takes a deep breath, before telling me about a near miss he had a hotel the day I was taken.

"Holy shit." I respond.

"I know."

Over the next twenty minutes, we go over my dad's *other* family. And then the kill shot comes.

"We also have to consider your mother, Raven."

"She didn't have anything to do with this." I automatically shut down. I don't want to talk about her and ruin this night.

"I don't think she did either, but she may have gotten into some sort of trouble and someone could be looking to hurt you to get back at her."

I'm shaking my head before he finishes his sentence. "I'd rather not talk about her."

"I'm sorry. I understand. I do need to let you know that Monica found her today and talked with her, though."

My nostrils flare and I feel my chest get thick. "She found her?"

"Yes, and she did ask her some questions about you. Your mom swore she didn't have to do anything with this, and Monica felt like she was being truthful but we can't mark her off just yet. She also asked if she could contact you to check on you herself."

"Fuck."

"We told her that it was your call, and that we'd relay the message to you. Monica said your mom acted like she understood."

"Was she…is she any better?" I bring myself to ask.

His pause tells me everything I need to know.

"Never mind, don't answer that," I say. "I'd rather not speak with her. Could you please let Monica know I'd rather not have any contact with her?"

"Of course."

I burrow my head into his chest and ask if we can be done with this for tonight. He agrees and I feel him drifting off to sleep a little while after.

I try to wipe my eyes, praying he can't feel the wet spot on his shirt, not wanting him to know I've been crying. I sit up and roll over, turning my back to the now sleeping man beside me.

A few seconds later I feel the mattress dip and a tissue appears over my shoulder.

He knew the whole time, but he didn't try to comfort me. He pretended to be asleep.

I think I love him.

Fifty

Emmett

When I'm sure Raven is actually asleep and not silently crying anymore, I roll over and check my phone for messages from Monica.

But I got nothing. They say no news is good news, however, waiting has never been my strongest skillset.

I roll back over and pull Raven closer to my chest, spooning her and burying my face into the back of her neck. I breathe her in, committing her scent to memory.

What the fuck is wrong with you, man?

I just can't get enough of this woman.

The sound of my phone ringing beside the bed wakes me and I see that it's around four AM.

I scramble to grab it from the nightstand before it wakes Raven. "Detective Fisher."

"Hey, it's Tropp. I found Lacey, I'm bringing her into the station."

"Goddamn, Monica, did you go home at all?"

"Yeah, I was asleep but one of my leads got back in touch with me and had eyes on her, so I just picked her up."

"I'll meet you there." I hang up and slide out of the bed gently.

"Everything okay?" Raven sleepily asks without opening her eyes.

"Yes, gorgeous. I'm going to the station to interview Lacey. The security guys are downstairs. I'll be back as soon as possible." I lean down and kiss her forehead.

She lets out a little sigh in response and she's back asleep before I'm fully dressed.

At the bottom of her little hidden doorway, there's one guard I haven't met yet, then there's another one at the back entrance. I stop for a second to chat with the one at the base of the stairs, whose name tag says Arnold, to let him know where I'm going and to call me if anything happens.

I quickly walk to my car and get in. Looking around, I don't see anyone. I'm probably just anxious about interviewing Lacey and what kind of information we'll get out of her. I send another thank you to the skies for Elli providing the security detail for Raven, otherwise there's no way I could leave her side.

I call Tropp back on my way to the station and let her know I'll be there in ten, and she tells me that, so far, Lacey isn't speaking.

I make it there in six minutes and bound up the steps into the station. I wave hello to the receptionist that's already there before heading downstairs to the basement floor, where I run into Alex again.

"Hey, man. Monica asked me to help out with the interview. Are you cool with that?"

I eye him for a moment before answering, "Sure. Fine with me."

It is his shift, after all, and even though Monica and I are the ones on the case, everyone is chipping in where they can.

My personal issues with Alex were just over a week ago, but honestly, it feels like a year has passed. So much has happened and I'm over it. We have bigger fish to fry— and Alex is a damn good interrogator, even if it pains me to admit that.

We continue down to the basement floor where the interview rooms are. There are six, although I think we could've gotten away with one. This town rarely has crime—one of the reasons I chose to move here. My job as a detective is needed, but I'm not so overwhelmed with work and bogged down with cases that I'm getting burnt out.

There are three rooms on each side of the hallway, and as we reach the bottom of the stairs I see Monica leaning against the door frame of room four.

"How's it going?" I ask her.

"Waited for you. I figured giving her some time to stew and get nervous could only benefit us. She hasn't asked for a lawyer. I don't think she thinks she needs one. So for right now, everything is fair game," Monica says.

I hear heels clicking down the hallway and glance up to see our lead psychologist, Stacey Jennings. She's coming toward us and I give her a nod, thankful she's here to profile and help us assess Lacey to figure out the best course of action with her interview.

Monica briefs her on the case while I look over the file with Alex, making sure he's up-to-date on what's going on. We decide that Alex and I will go in first and try to rattle her a little, and Stacey and Monica will watch the live feed from a nearby room. Stacey will assess what she sees, then she and Monica will go in to see if they can get any more from Lacey.

I take deep breath and look over at Alex, who gives me a curt nod.

It's go time.

Fifty-One

Raven

My alarm goes off at six AM and I bury my head under my pillow.

It's Thursday. The shop doesn't open until ten but it's shipment day, and the new stock will be coming in around eight.

Groaning, I roll out of bed and catch myself looking around for Emmett before remembering he went into the station at some point during the night. I fire off a text to him to let him know I'm awake and wish him luck before I jump in the shower. The scent of my apple and pear shampoo makes me grin. Emmett's been using it since he doesn't have his own toiletries here and the smell reminds me of him. I guess I should get him some toiletries of his own. he's been here every single night since we met, except the night we stayed at my father's—together.

I put that idea back on the shelf, the thought of him having items here freaking me out a little. *I know it doesn't mean he's moving in, but that's the first step, isn't it?* Staying over often, then leaving a few outfits just in case you need them, and then toiletries, and then all of a sudden you have a new roommate.

Yeah, let's definitely shelve that for now.

Another thing I don't want to think about: I'm supposed to have lunch with my dad today.

I have so many questions for him and yet part of me doesn't want to know. *What made him choose his wife and sons over my mother if she really was the love of his life?*

He loved her enough to get a tattoo for her—something I'm sure his wife doesn't know the true meaning behind. He said it was because of his career, and I guess I understand that, but I can admit it stings a little. As much as I don't want to rehash everything, I do think getting answers will help me decide where we go from here.

I get out of the shower and grab my big fluffy white towel from the bar on the wall beside me, drying off quickly and wrapping it around myself before grabbing my phone from the counter. There's a text from Emmett that I start reading as I step back into the main area of my loft.

I hear a throat clear and let out a yelp, slinging my phone in the process. "What the fuck—"

One of the night-time security guards spins around so his back is to me, and because he's bald I can see the blush that's reached his ears and the back of his head. He's red as a beet.

"I'm so sorry, Miss Jackson, I was told to check in with you every hour once Detective Fisher left. I've peeked up here twice and you were asleep. I didn't mean to startle you."

I take a deep breath and calm my anger before responding, "It's completely fine. Thank you for doing your job. I'm fine, though. If you could please wait downstairs, I'll be down shortly."

"Yes m'am." He scurries to the door, still keeping his back to me and fumbling to grab ahold of the banister.

I almost laugh at the absurdity of the situation.

I have freaking bodyguards. Who have to check on me hourly when my detective "boyfriend" isn't here.

Thank God I didn't waltz out here naked like I usually do.

He's just doing his job. He's just doing his job.

I repeat my mantra to myself while getting dressed in one of my Poe's tees and favorite ripped jeans, and by the time my hair is curled in loose waves down my back and my makeup is finished, I'm grinning to myself at how red that guard's ears were and how quickly he scrambled back down the steps.

If I have to deal with this less-than-ideal situation, I might as well have fun with it.

Fifty-Two

Emmett

The room is completely silent, save for the sound of tapping feet against linoleum tile. Lacey's hair is a hot-red mane around her face, and something in her eyes isn't quite right. Like a cat who already ate the mouse. We've been in here for hours, rotating out and trying to get her break.

"All right, Miss Carter. I just need you to tell us what you know," Alex says, trying yet again to get her to talk.

She looks up at him and a giggle escapes her lips before she puts her hand over her mouth. "Sorry!"

I see Alex's eyes squint a little, and I'm with him. This is not what we were expecting, her show is either a ploy or we need Stacey in here sooner rather than later.

"Lacey." At my tone her eyes dart to mine, and the light dancing there sets me on edge. "What do you know about what happened to Raven and Elliott?"

She shrugs her shoulders and looks back at the table, like a child who'd just been scorned.

"We just need information, Lacey," I say, softer. "We know you didn't do anything, but you know who did, don't you?"

"I do."

"Can you tell us?"

Another giggle. "It's not whoever you think it is. I know, but you don't." Her hand covers her mouth again and her eyes dart around the room.

"Is it funny, Lacey? What happened to Elliott James, is that funny to you?" Alex's voice is firm.

"Well, I'm not sure, *detective*. I don't think that was in the plans."

Alex meets my gaze over her head, both of us still standing—Alex, leaning his arms on the table beside her, and me, propped up against the wall. We can't both crowd her, risking her shutting down, but one of us needs to look aggressive.

"What plan?" he asks her.

She shakes her head, eyes wide.

"Lacey, you can be in a lot of trouble, you know. You're an accessory in this. Someone was hurt, and you know who did this. You can tell us, or you can deal with the consequences," Alex says.

It seems like he's losing his patience and I'm right there with him.

She has the sense to look surprised before smirking again. With a shrug, she goes back to staring at her hands.

I lock eyes with Alex again, nodding toward the door.

He taps the desk twice and steps back.

"All right, Lacey. We'll be back shortly," I say to her.

The door clicks behind us and I make sure I don't comment until we're across the hall in the room with Monica and Stacey, where they've been watching the camera footage.

"What in the actual fuck?" Monica is rubbing her eyes.

"She's cracked," I state, shaking my head.

"It's like dealing with a fucking five-year-old. Can we hold her here?" Alex asks, looking at Monica.

"Captain is working on it," she replies, checking her phone.

Someone clears their throat and we stop our banter to look over at Monica and Stacey. "What did you guys think?" I ask.

Alex plops down in the seat across from Stacey and I follow suit.

Stacey gestures toward the screen. "Look at her."

"Yeah, the same shit she was doing in there," Alex says, blowing out his breath.

We're all exhausted.

"No, Alex, really look at her," Stacey insists.

I follow his gaze and study the girl on the screen. Her vibrant green cardigan contrasting against her mess of wild red hair. The edges frayed, clearly worn out. The nail polish on her fingers is chipped, and she's chewing on one of her thumbs. I can see by the table shaking that she's still bouncing her leg.

"She looks anxious," Alex states.

Stacey nods.

"Okay but wouldn't anyone be? She's in a police station for questioning. Does she look crazy right now?" Alex asks.

"No." Stacey rewinds the footage to a few minutes prior, when we had entered the interrogating room.

We watch as Lacey's entire demeanor changes as the door opens. The wild look in her eyes isn't there, but the second the door opens for us, it is and her bouncing increases.

"She's trying to make us think she's lost it," Alex says blandly.

"I believe so. Either because she thinks her punishment will be less severe if she can prove she wasn't of sound mind, or because she's trying to throw us off on what's really going on here," Stacey confirms.

"So what do we do now?" I finally ask.

"Now we try." Monica's answer is strong and confident.

I shoot her a forced smile and hope that she and Stacey can get further than Alex and I did.

Fifty-Three

Raven

I hear the ding over the door and turn to see Reggie coming in. It's a little after eleven and he looks disheveled.

"Everything all right?" I ask him.

"Yeah, sorry I'm late. I just left the police department, and let me tell you, I never want to do that again, honey. Only for you."

"Shit. They called you in?"

"Yeah, they just wanted to know about Lacey. How she was when she was here, what sort of relationship I had with her, and if she had made any strange comments about you."

"And you told them about the weird vibes and all?" I ask him.

He nods, blowing air out of puffed cheeks. "Yep. They didn't tell me anything, but I do know she's still there so that's got to mean something."

"Do you think I could have actually had someone working for me that was feeding information to some sort of enemy?"

"You didn't even know there *was* an enemy, Rave."

"I know, but it creeps me out regardless."

"And it should. But you've got these handy dandy hunky security men surrounding you, plus a drop-dead gorgeous cop at your every beck and call. I could barely hold it together in the same room with him at the station. I'm not sure how you don't jump—" he pauses, noticing said cop's presence and adds—oh hey, Emmett."

I spin around and see Emmett grinning slyly, leaning against the door frame to the stock room.

Reggie is seven shades redder than I've ever seen him and I start giggling uncontrollably. Emmett's green eyes flash with laughter before he joins me, and then all three of us are clutching our sides and gasping for breath. With how tense things have been, it's a much-needed release.

When I finally calm down enough to make a complete sentence, I tell Reggie I'm heading out for lunch with my dad, and we all sober up at the thought.

"Maybe you should make a list of things you want to ask," Reggie suggests. "Stay on track and don't let your emotions get involved. Get those answers and you can assess it all later, you know?"

I nod in agreement and grab a pad of paper and pen to make a list as Emmett drives me to a steakhouse on the outskirts of town.

What do *I want to ask my father?*

I start to write, thankful Emmett is giving me the silence I need to think.

- Where is the wife? Still around?
- More about my half-brothers
- Did you ever see me after I was born?
- When is the last time you had contact with my mother?
- Discuss money situation, no more checks

I tap the pen against my chin.

As much as I want answers, he doesn't owe any to me. He made his choices, all those years ago, and in his own way he's been trying to make up for it.

I'm resolved as we pull into the parking lot of the restaurant, where I see my father leaning against his truck, waiting for us.

I didn't peg him for a truck guy. The truck throws off the entire persona I've created in my head for him.

He's wearing khaki dress pants and a red short-sleeve golf shirt, even though it's forty degrees outside.

Maybe a product of living at the coast.

His salt and pepper hair is parted on the side and slicked over, much like Emmett's, so he stays with the times. He does have two sons, so I guess that makes sense.

Emmett parks, gets out and shakes his hand, and tells my father he'll see him shortly, then leaves us there.

My entourage had followed behind us in a separate vehicle, and now, they're following us inside.

Phil and Mark are back, the night-shift having went home around nine this morning. I never caught their names, and I make a mental note to ask them tonight. Mark heads off to case the building and man the entrances, and Phil stays with us, sitting at a table directly behind us where he can see me at all times. It's annoying, but I can't deny that I'm comforted by them being here.

Looking across the table at the man sitting there makes my breath catch. So many of my own features are staring back at me, and though this isn't the first time I've laid eyes on him, this feels like the first time I've been able to study his features.

Suddenly my list of questions isn't my first priority. "Tell me about you. Tell me what I should know about my father."

The shock and then instant relief that floods his face almost brings a tear to my eye.

Almost.

Fifty-Four

Emmett

"Fisher," I answer.

"We're finished." The annoyance in Monica's voice tells me what I need to know.

I pull out of the restaurant parking lot, heading back to the station. "Anything?"

"Not much. She did indicate that there's someone else behind the entire scheme, and that Brent is a hired player just like she is, but we knew that already."

I blow out a breath, steeling my frustration. "Better to have confirmation, though."

"She asked for a lawyer," Monica adds.

Shit.

"Perfect."

"The fact that we have one of the players might rattle them. Someone is going to fuck up, Em. It's going to come out. Stay close to Raven."

"I just dropped her off to have lunch with her dad. He's coming in afterwards to give his statement."

"Okay. I'll wait for you and we can brief the captain together."

I end the call and resist banging my head against the steering wheel.

We're going to catch them.
I try to convince myself of it.

After we've given the captain our report on Lacey's interview, we're back in the conference room going over our notes.

"She said she knows, but we don't. I just have a hunch this is someone that we haven't even considered or interviewed. She was toying with us, like she knows we're way off," I say, trying to work through it out loud.

Monica nods and I rub my hands over my face.

A knock at the door tells us that Raven's dad is here for his interview.

We shuffle out of the conference room and he's standing in the waiting area with Susan, no Raven in sight. Not that I thought she'd accompany him, but part of me had hoped to see her.

Fucking goner.

"All right, Mr. Jackson, we just need to ask you a few questions on the record to get your account of the night of the kidnapping and also clear you as a suspect for the attack on Elliott James," Monica tells him.

She's leading the interview while I observe and take notes.

Robert nods at her to continue.

"Can you state your name and how you know Raven Jackson?"

"Robert Cole Jackson. I am Raven's biological father."

"Perfect, and can you tell us what happened two nights ago?"

He looks down at his hands sheepishly and gives Monica a full recount of what occurred. Afterwards, he looks up at Monica, like he's ready to defend his actions.

She nods at him encouragingly. "Do you know anyone who may want to hurt your daughter?"

"No, but like I said, I haven't been present in her life. I just recently found out that her mother isn't in her life either."

They spend a few minutes rehashing the reason Robert wasn't there to be a father to her, and then Monica asks the kicker. "Does your wife know about Raven?"

Robert takes a deep breath and nods. "I finally told her about a year ago. I'm not proud that I kept her a secret for so long, but that's the truth."

"And your sons, do they know?" she asks him.

He nods again.

"How did your wife react to the news?" she prods.

"She was upset, understandably. More-so that I wasn't taking responsibility for my daughter and that I had abandoned her. It surprised me. I honestly thought she would divorce me over this, and here she was, more angry at me for *not* telling her, which kept us from being a part of Raven's life. She wants to meet Raven. She's been nagging me since she found out to make contact with Raven and tell her about her brothers. She wants her to be a part of our family." He smiles a small smile and looks off into the distance, likely remembering his wife's reaction.

My ears perk up at this, and I stare at him incredulously. "Wow."

He gives me that same half-smile that I've seen often on Raven's face countless times. "I didn't tell her how I thought Raven's mom was my soulmate. As far as she knows, it was an office fling that ended with an unwanted pregnancy."

"Understandable." Monica puts her hand on his forearm and looks at him warmly, and I think we've both concluded that we can mark Robert and his wife off as suspects.

It just doesn't fit.

We wrap up the interview and I clap Robert on the back. "I think you've got a shot at this family thing. It may take her some time, but I think you'll get there."

I think I see a tear in his eye as he shakes my hand and heads back down the hallway, but it's gone as fast as it came, leaving me unsure if I imagined it.

Fifty-Five

Raven

"So how'd it go?" Reggie is standing over in the corner of the shop, straightening and fluffing the pillows on the bench there.

"It was… interesting. There's so much I didn't know. He's still married. His wife wants me to come over for dinner when I'm comfortable, which could be never."

"Oh come on, Raven. Everyone needs a family. He fucked up, sure, but you have two brothers and a stepmom who want to be in your life, you know? Don't waste it. Not everyone has a family. This is your chance at one."

I'm surprised at the passion in his voice, but I know he lost his parents when he was really young. That's sort of why we fit together so well—two misfits without a family coming together to be there for each other. Same with Missy and Jason, because their families live in California. We've all come to be our own little family.

"I know. And I'm going to try, I promise. It's just a lot to wrap my head around right now."

He nods at me and makes his way to the storage room to finish the end-of-day tasks.

I'm going through our sales for today and comparing them to last year. We're up thirty percent. The bookstore is growing, and people are starting to use it as a hangout as well as a place to find their favorite authors.

I feel such a sense of pride as I look around this place. Rows and rows of books, a comfy sitting area, a few loaner shelves for those who can't afford to buy books right now. I have framed art on the walls—pictures of ravens, a portrait of Edgar Allen Poe. The entire back wall is painted white, with the words of the poem "The Raven" painted across the entire wall.

It's perfect. It's everything I've always pictured.

My phone dings and it's a text from Emmett letting me know he's stopping by the burger joint down the road on his way home and asking what I want. I quickly respond and hit send, thankful that he's on his way. It's been an emotionally draining day all around, and I'm anxious to find out if they got anything from Lacey.

I feel myself smiling as Reggie comes back into the main area with his satchel, waiting for Todd to pull up. Since the attack, Todd doesn't want Reggie leaving on his own, so he's been picking him up every night. I can't say I blame him.

Reggie comes up and wraps his arms around me in a bear hug. "It's been a rough bit, huh, love?"

I nod against his shoulder and resist the urge to cry. I don't get emotional, so it would surely freak Reggie out to see me crack.

"I think you're coming out if it, Rave. New man, new family, Elli of course, thriving bookstore. You're going to be just fine. They're going to catch him soon. They have to."

I sniffle a little and thank him just as Todd is pulling up. Mark escorts Reggie out while Phil stays by my side.

I go upstairs, making sure I have my panic button, and change into my PJs to wait for Emmett to get home.

Home.

Fifty-Six

Raven's fingernails trail over my back as we lie in her bed, my head in her lap. The sound of pages turning as she reads echoes throughout the loft.

I can't remember the last time I felt this at peace.

"Emmett?"

"Yeah?" I turn in her lap so that I'm looking up at her.

"This is nice."

I wait, expecting more to follow, but she goes back to reading.

I'm not sure if we just had some sort of breakthrough or what, but I'll take it. I'm still turned facing upwards to her, and I can see a subtle blush highlighting her high cheekbones. I want to make a joke to put her at ease, but I don't. I just nod in agreement and keep watching her.

She's ignoring me, like she doesn't want to admit any more than she already just did.

But, I can feel those walls slowly coming down.

The next morning I decide to take the captain's advice and stay close to Raven throughout the day, unless we get another lead to follow.

There have been no sightings of Brent Smallwood since the attempted kidnapping. No hospitals have any record of anyone coming in with injuries consistent to a car wreck, and he hasn't returned to the hotel, although they're still holding the room and charging the card on file.

The same card that was used at the bar the night this all started.

Lacey is still being held but hasn't given any more info.

I hear Raven's phone ringing from her side of the bed, but she's in the shower and I don't answer it because I don't think it's my place, nor do I think she'd appreciate it.

A few minutes later she emerges in a cloud of steam, wrapped in a towel. Her wet hair is dripping down her back, leaving a trail of water on the floor as she walks over to me.

I lose all train of thought as she leans down over the bed, dropping the towel as she does so.

"You have some spare time, Detective Fisher?"

I nod.

"Perfect," she says.

I'm out of my boxers and reaching for a condom before she can blink, and she's giggling at my excitement.

"Don't." She stills my hand from rolling it on and I toss it to the side.

I guess after the other night she's decided we don't need them, and I'm fine with that if she is.

She lies back on the bed and I take a second to look at her.

She really is the most beautiful thing I've ever seen. Her body is perfect. Her long black hair is soaking wet and splayed out over her head. The scent of her shampoo fills the air as I lean in and hover over her body. I kiss her neck, down to her collarbone and farther, living for her small gasps.

"Emmett."

"Hmmm?" I continue my descent as she squirms beneath me.

"I need you to hurry."

"Oh?" I lift my head and look at her, the fire burning in her green eyes making it hard to restrain myself.

"Please."

I continue to make my way down, slower than before, and I hear an impatient noise escape her lips. I let out a chuckle and she squeezes her eyes shut so she can't see me grinning at her.

"Emmett," she pleads.

And I give her what she wants—over and over again.

Afterwards, we're lying across the bed; her still-damp hair is an unruly mess and I run my fingers through it.

Her phone starts to ring again.

"Shit," I say. "I'm sorry. I meant to tell you it was ringing earlier when you were in the shower."

"That's all right," she says, giving me another grin. "You were a little busy."

I smack her ass as she rolls across me to get to her phone.

She's giggling, but stops when she sees the caller ID. "It's Landry's mom."

Wrenn Montgomery

Fifty-Seven

Raven

"Hello?" I answer.

"Raven! Hi, darling!"

"Hi, Mrs. Davis. How are you?" I know she knows what I'm asking, which is how she is doing after the death of her son.

"I was wondering if you'd want to grab dinner tonight? Catch up? Let me take you out on the town. My treat," she says.

I pause for a second, caught off guard.

I haven't seen or talked to her in five years, but before everything with Landry happened, we were close. Not like a mother and daughter, but almost like friends.

We went to dinner often, went shopping, I'd attend her charity events as her plus-one if her husband Jay couldn't attend.

Dinner with her might be nice. And I know she's hurting right now. She probably wants to meet up to see me, to remember Landry for who he was before everything went to shit for him.

I'm sure Emmett wouldn't tag along because of how fucking awkward that would be, but one of the bodyguards most likely would.

"Sure!" I finally decide on. "Where and what time?"

"I'll come pick you up, say seven-ish? Do you want to try that new seafood place in Iverson?"

Iverson is about a half hour away, but I've heard of the place she's referring to and I do want to try it.

"I'll just meet you there," I tell her. "No need for you to go out of your way to meet me. I'll see you around seven."

"Well, all right, dear! I'll see you then!"

We hang up and I glance over at Emmett, who's trying to give me my space without eavesdropping, but it's hard in a loft apartment.

"She wants me to meet her for dinner tonight," I inform him.

"That'll be nice."

He sounds like he truly means it, and I think of how that speaks to his emotional maturity. To be okay with me—*his girlfriend (?)*—going out to dinner with my dead ex-boyfriend's mom and not batting an eye about it just shows that he trusts me to make the right decisions for myself.

This is nothing like Landry's jealous rage.

"Yeah, I think so. I mean, it'll be awkward for sure. Five years of pent-up feelings and I'm sure she's mourning. I think it'll be good for her."

"Maybe it'll be good for you, too," he says.

"Maybe."

"All the stock from yesterday's delivery has been shelved. Did you see that new Jamie Foster release? That fucking cover, I could eat him up."

"Reggie."

"I'm just saying. He's a fictional model, Raven. Jesus. Don't tell Todd." Reggie pretends to fan himself, dropping into one of the chairs in the reading corner.

I chuckle and tell him, "The designer sent over some proofs for the new T-shirts. Look at these." I walk over to him and show him my iPad, and we decide together on which colors and designs to restock.

I really should make him partner. It's something I've been contemplating for a while. He loves this place as much as I do.

Phil is back for the day-shift, and he's hovering near the checkout counter, keeping a watch on the front door and us. Mark is somewhere outside of the building, probably in the back. I'm guessing one of them will stay here while I go to dinner with Elizabeth tonight, and one will go with me.

"I'm going to dinner with Landry's mom tonight."

"Like your ex in prison, Landry?"

"That's the one, except he was killed a few weeks ago." His jaw drops, and I keep going. "I think she's mourning. I mean of course she is. She called and wanted to go to dinner, and I feel like I owe her that much. I did put her son in prison." I'm picking at the rug beneath me, where I've plopped down on the floor to sort books.

"Excuse me, you did not put her son in prison. You ratted him out, sure."

I give him a look.

"I mean you did, but that's what you should have done, and you were trying to save a life. He killed someone, Raven, whether he pulled the trigger or not. He orchestrated it. Don't feel guilty."

"I know, that's what Elli said, too."

"Elli's a smart cookie. Does she know you're going to dinner with his mom?"

"Not yet. I'm dreading telling her. You know how she gets."

"You better tell her, Raven, *before* you go tonight. I know she's feeling out of the loop over there cooped up in her apartment."

"Another thing I feel guilty about," I say under my breath.

"I'm going to smack you over the head with one of these," he says, waving a book in the air.

Phil pops his head up from the front, eyebrows raised.

"Not really," Reggie tells him. "Calm down, Cujo."

I chuckle, knowing he's right. I need to call Elli and tell her what's going on.

Better yet…

"Can you hold it down here while I take her some lunch?" I ask Reggie.

"You want to tell her in person? You brave, brave soul. But yes, I'll hold it down here." He rolls his eyes but gives me a grin.

"You're the best."

"Don't I know it, babe."

Fifty-Eight

Emmett

The mirror is foggy by the time I step out of the shower, having taken the time in the steam to sort through my feelings about the case. We're getting nowhere with Lacey, and we have no other leads.

How the fuck does someone just drop off the face of the Earth?

There's been no sign of Brent Smallwood since the attempted kidnapping. No other leads. No tips.

I finish getting dressed and head downstairs to find Raven. When I reach the bottom of her stairs I can hear her muffled laughter through the hidden door and I catch myself grinning at the sound of it. She has so much on her plate right now, between her own life being in danger, her best friend being attacked, finding out who her father is, the strain of her non-relationship with her mother, plus finding out about Landry's death, yet here she is giggling in the middle of her bookstore with her friend.

Pushing the door open, my eyes find her immediately. Head thrown back, eyes shining with happiness, her long black hair falling in waves down her back. My breath catches. I've known hundreds of women in my lifetime, and I've told many of them they were beautiful, whispered it to them while they were in my bed, threw the compliment out like it was weightless. But in this moment, I realize I'd been a liar. "Beautiful" doesn't seem like a strong enough word to describe Raven, but if that's what she is, every other woman has paled in comparison.

Her eyes find me and her grin widens. "Hey you. Have a good shower?"

"Would've been better if you had joined me."

Reggie turns a little pink and backs away toward the stock room as I walk through the shelves to her. "On that note," he says, and disappears through the doorway.

"I'll make a note for next time," she says as she wraps her arms around my neck, pulling me down to where she had just been sitting on the floor. "Sit with me?"

I shake my head, pushing away the thoughts of having my way with her in the middle of the bookstore. We'll have to save that for another time, like when the store is closed and there aren't bodyguards and an employee lurking nearby.

"Do you need help with these?" I gesture toward the pile of books she's sorting.

"If you don't mind. I just need to sort them by genre. I want to feature them up front and get it done before I go take Elli lunch."

"She still isn't really leaving her apartment, huh?" I ask her.

Phil told me yesterday that Elli had only left her apartment the one night to come here, when she found out Raven was missing. Other than that, she's been holed up in her penthouse.

"Yeah, I don't know what to do. I know she's worried, of course she is. And the trauma...I don't know. She's having sessions with a psych friend of mine and she says they're going well but who knows. I'm going over there so I can tell her I'm going to dinner with Elizabeth, Landry's mom, and spend some time with her. I may get ready there."

"I think that's a good idea. It'd be good for her to feel some normalcy again, like things were before this all started. I'm gonna go to the station and check in with Monica, but I'll be around if you need me."

Her hands move swiftly through the stack of books, sorting them faster than I can read the titles. "Thank you."

"I thought I could help you with this." I chuckle, as she's almost already done. "Want me to start carrying them to the front for you?"

"Yes, please. Just set them on the front shelves and I'll come organize them when I'm done sorting. Thank you again, for everything, not just the book help." She winks at me then goes right back to sorting.

"You're welcome, gorgeous." I gather the stacks and carry them up to the front, hearing her give a humph and grinning as I go.

Wrenn Montgomery

Fifty-Nine

Raven

The giant gold doors close on me again, showing my reflection. Hair curled in gentle waves, faded jeans and a Poe's hoodie, not unlike that morning a few weeks ago when my entire life changed.

But the eyes. My eyes are a night and day difference from the girl on that panic-stricken morning. Gone are the frantic, teary, terrified eyes. In their place staring back at me are glowing, radiant, *happy* eyes.

Eyes that belong to a woman in love.

And though there's still a sliver of terror there and also sadness for the chain of events that got me here, I'm grateful. Amidst all this chaos, I somehow fell in love.

The ding of the doors opening on Elli's floor draws me out of my musing and I take in her foyer. Neat as a pin, no shoes strewn about, no sign of a struggle.

I shake my head clear and walk to her door, wondering if I'll ever be able to come here without thinking about that morning.

"Get in here, bitch." Elli throws the door open, tapping her foot as I meander through the doorway. "You haven't been in a hurry a day in your life, have you?"

"Why am I hurrying?"

"I have a one o'clock coming."

"A client? Coming here?" I ask her.

"You could say that." She has the grace to look sheepish as she closes the door behind me.

"Elliott." I know good and well she's not letting a client come to her personal home.

"What? I have needs, Raven. Needs! And I haven't had sex since…you know." She dismisses it with a wave of her hand, and I cringe.

"You're just going to keep calling it 'you know'? You were raped, Elli. And I'm not saying you're not ready, only you can decide that, but if you're doing this as a distraction from dealing with—"

"I don't want to hear it. Honestly. I love you, I mean it, but mind your damn business."

My eyebrows shoot up, but I hold my tongue. I know this Elli—she's like a wounded animal. The closer you get to try to help, the more she'll maul you. "All right, all right. Who is he?"

She stares at me for a second longer, as if not really believing I'm letting it go, and I raise my eyebrows again pointedly.

"You going to show me his picture or just stand there?" The tension breaks as she twirls around looking for her phone. "Coffee table, E."

"I knew that. Okay, okay, so he's this new lawyer at the firm, and I know I shouldn't *but*…I can't say no. I mean look at him, Rave. Just look."

I grab her hand to hold her phone still so that I can look, and I see a handsome blond in a three-piece suit with a lazy smile. I wait for the stomach flip that usually comes with seeing a fine specimen of the opposite sex, but it doesn't come. He's attractive, sure, but he does nothing for me.

"He looks…lawyer-y," I say encouragingly to her, handing her phone back.

"That's it?"

I pull my lips in and nod.

"You're ruined," she states.

"Am not."

"Detective Emmett Fisher has ruined you," she says, shaking her head. "Can't say I blame you, though. If I was hitting that I'd only have eyes for him, too."

"Okay, enough. Come eat your lunch so I can leave before Mr. Lawyer gets here." I place the takeout containers on the coffee table and sit down on her white plush rug.

I try not to think about how destroyed her living room was that morning and push it out of my head.

She's redecorated—her way of pushing it out of hers.

I take my time opening my food, waiting until her mouth is full of her first bite of chicken parm before I drop the bomb. "I'm going to dinner with Landry's mom."

Chew. Chew. Chew. Eyes bulging. Gulp. "Excuse me?"

"She called this morning and said she wants to meet me for dinner. I think she's grieving, E. I just feel—"

"No, no. You don't feel sorry for her. You feel guilty and this is a guilt dinner and you have *no reason* to feel guilty. You may have tipped them off, but he would've been caught eventually. You just sped up the process before anyone else, including you, could have gotten hurt. You don't owe her a damn thing. When is the last time you heard from her? Five years ago? And now she wants to—"

"Elliott."

"Don't you *Elliott* me. I know you. If you want to go, you're going to go and that's that, but don't try to paint this as something it's not. You're only going because you feel responsible for her son getting killed and that's bullshit."

"You're probably right. But regardless, I told her I'm going so I'm going. I'll text you during and after. I just really do feel bad for her. I mean she lost the perfect image of him when he went to jail, and you know as well as I do that she spent that first year drunk and in bed. And now this. I don't know how she's going to cope. And no, it's not my responsibility, but at least I'll know that I did what I could. I don't plan on seeing her again after this. I just want to get it done and over with and move on from the Landry chapter."

"So you can move on to the Emmett one," she huffs.

I shoot her a stare and we both start giggling. "Not a bad chapter, if I say so myself. I was going to get ready here but since you're kicking me out for a dick appointment, I guess I'll go back to the shop and get ready there."

She rolls her eyes. "I'm not missing my appointment. Plus, I'm sure Reggie is dying to do your makeup."

It's my turn to roll my eyes, but I'm grinning as I head back to her elevator, ready to face this new chapter.

Sixty

Emmett

"Where the fuck have you been, bro?"

"Language." I hear the chuckle on the other end of the line. "I don't care if you're a badass Marine now or not. I've been busy," I say to my baby brother.

"Work got you slammed?" he asks.

"Something like that."

"Ooooh shit! It's a girl!"

I hear the excitement in his voice and bite back a grin. As the baby, Everette has always been the most dramatic of the three of us.

"Okay, okay, tell me about her," he says. "What's she look like?"

"I'm not telling you shit. You'll meet her when I'm good and ready to introduce her to your wild ass."

More chuckling and then, "You worried, big bro? Scared I might sweep her off her feet?"

"She'd chew you up and spit you out, Ev. In fact, you meeting her may be a good idea. Knock you down a few notches."

"I can't wait."

"Any news on your deployment?" I ask him.

At the question, his tone changes. "I've got about three weeks stateside then I'm out."

I take deep breath before I respond. It's part of the job, what we all signed up for. But since my injury last year, I've never worried more about my brothers. Getting shot made it real for me. I'm not invincible, and neither are they. It's his first deployment and that's always the hardest one.

"All right. I really do have some work stuff going on, but I want to fly out to see you before you ship out," I tell him.

"Sounds good, bro. Bring your girl."

"We'll see."

"Don't be scared, I won't steal her away. I mean I can't help it if she wants—"

"Everette."

Cackling laughter.

"I'll talk to you soon, you little shit," I tell him.

"Love you, bro," he says.

"Love you too, man."

I end the call and rest my head against the steering wheel for a few beats.

Pull it together, Emmett.

It's our way of life. Just because he's the baby doesn't mean you need to get all emotional.

I take a deep breath and get out of the car, heading into the station to check in with Monica and see if we have any new leads, although I know we don't. She would've called if we did.

Something needs to happen soon. Maybe we need to re-interview Lacey and be a little harsher this time.

I put a call out to Stacey to have her call me when she can.

Time to play hardball.

Sixty-One

Raven

"I really should've made her pick a different restaurant."

"Oh stop fussing. Close your eyes. Now blink," Reggie demands.

There's only an hour left until I'm supposed to meet Elizabeth and I'm already regretting this.

I usually do my own makeup, but Reggie always begs to do my eyes so tonight I'm letting him. We've had three customers wander in. One of them stopped to comment on the shade of eyeshadow Reggie was using. The other two ignored us, likely having been here before and knowing this is not that unusual here. You never know what you'll get at Poe's.

"She's boujie as hell. Let her treat you to a nice restaurant instead of those burgers Emmett's been bringing you every night. Live a little."

"How about you mind your damn business about what I eat?" I joke.

"So touchy. Okay, look in the mirror."

I do as he says, and I have to admit, he's outdone himself yet again. I'd suggest he be a professional makeup artist, but I can't have him leaving the shop. My green eyes look like polished jade stones, the browns and golds he's used for the eyeshadow making them pop. My lashes are so long, if I blink quick enough, I may actually take flight. "Wow."

"Mm hmm, thought so. Now go finish your hair and put your dress on. Text me when you're about to come down so I can be ready for the grand entrance."

I roll my eyes again but hop off the stool and head upstairs. There's a note on top of the dress I laid across my bed earlier.

I can't wait to take this off of you tonight.

-E

I pick it up, grinning, and tuck it into my desk drawer with my other keepsakes.

Forty-five minutes later, I'm dressed and ready to go meet Elizabeth. Mark is going to stay at the shop with Reggie and keep an eye on the shop, and Phil will ride with me. I try not to cringe at the thought. I don't mind Phil as much anymore, and when this shit is solved, I may even be sad to see him go. However, I won't be sad about getting my independence back.

I call Emmett to check in and let him know I'm about to leave, but it goes to voicemail. A few minutes later I get a text saying they're working on interviewing Lacey again and he'll probably be home late.

I run to the public restroom downstairs, spin around, and snap a photo of my ass in my dress to send to him, knowing he'll be speeding later to get home as soon as he can.

I giggle as a few dings go off in my purse where I'd just stashed my phone. He'll have to wait until we get there for me to reply. It'll drive him crazy.

I say goodbye to Reggie and shoot Mark a warning look before I go, but I know I don't have to worry. He'll keep my employee safe.

The drive doesn't take as long as I expected, probably because I let Phil control the playlist and I'm pleasantly surprised by his choice of music. We pull up to the fancy restaurant, stopping at the valet and handing him the keys to my very average car amongst all these very expensive ones.

I hear heels click up behind me and instantly know it's her.

Deep breath, Raven. Deep breath. You can do this.

I spin to greet her. "Mrs. Davis!"

My eyes land on her and I take her in. It may have been years since I've seen her, but she hasn't aged a day—no doubt thanks to the best plastic surgeons in North Carolina. She's wearing a navy skirt and blazer, with a string of large pearls around her neck. Her shoulder-length blonde hair is perfectly styled, and her heels are still clicking across the cement as she approaches.

But her eyes are dead.

"Oh, Raven! Look at you!" She places her hands on both of my arms, looking over me like she's inspecting me. "I love that dress!"

"Thank you. You look great, as always!"

"Psh," she says, waving a hand, "I've seen better days."

I ignore the comment, not wanting to go where that's headed. I motion to the maître d' and ask, "Ready?"

Sixty-Two

Emmett

A knock on my door has me looking up from the paperwork on my desk, and I'm relieved to see it's Stacey. I gesture for her to come in and she does so and sits down, a file in her hands.

"We need to crack her," I say. "I know we've been playing nice, but I'm done with that now. We have no other leads, we have nowhere else to go with this. We're just sitting ducks waiting for him to attack again."

"I agree, and I've been studying her case file. I think we need to go in with a disciplinary tone. She has several markers in her chart that indicate she's susceptible to authority figures, and I believe you and Alex weren't intimidating enough. The approach Monica and I took was much too soft. I would assume whoever has hired her to work for them has figured this out about her. She answers to them not because she wants to, but because she needs the structure. She feels included. If we can go in like we're ashamed that she would betray Raven by doing this to her and make her feel like one of the family members in Raven's clique, we can establish a disciplinary tone and it may make her cave."

"I'm on board with that, but I think it should be Alex who goes in and lays it down. She knows I'm involved and she won't tell me anything."

"Okay but if that doesn't work, it may need to be you who goes in pleadingly."

"That's our last resort," I say.

"Agreed."

"Let me get Monica in here and we can go over a plan. Then we'll go talk to Captain Harrison together. We also need to alert her lawyer and get the paperwork together," I tell her.

She nods, and I shoot a text over to Monica.

"So, and I'm sorry for prying, but you and Raven Jackson?" she asks.

I lift my head from my phone, and say, "What about it?"

"I just," she starts, blushing, looking a little flustered, "I didn't know you were on the market."

Oh.

Shit.

"Ha, well, I wasn't looking, but it sort of fell into my lap right before this case started and we've gotten pretty serious."

"That's fast."

I lift an eyebrow.

"I mean…gah, I didn't mean that in a bad way. I know Raven, through the Psychology field, and she's an awesome person. Complex, but awesome. I think you guys are great together. I'm sorry if it sounded otherwise. I have to admit I've had a crush on you for a while." She bends her head to hide her blush. "But I think you've found a great match, and I'm happy for you."

I'm taken aback. I can usually tell when someone is flirting with me or trying to get my attention, but I've never felt that from Stacey. "I appreciate your honesty. She is pretty damn awesome."

Monica knocks on the door, saving the day.

I owe her another coffee.

"So we've got a new game plan?" she asks, plopping down in the seat beside Stacey, adequately breaking the tension that had crowded the room.

Wrenn Montgomery

Sixty-Three

Raven

We enter the restaurant and I'm taken aback by the luxuriousness of it, but what did I expect? This is Elizabeth Davis we're dealing with.

The hostess begins to lead us to our table, and Phil asks to be seated close to us, but Elizabeth interrupts him.

"Actually, I've reserved a special room for us," she says. "You know how I hate being distracted during my meals, and with all the press lately…"

She puts a hand over her mouth, as if to stifle a cry and I eye her, turning to Phil to whisper, "Do you think you could just wait outside the door for us? I mean, she's harmless." I motion toward her and give him a smile. "She's grieving, and she's been through enough, you know? I'll have the emergency alert button. I'll press it if anything happens, I promise."

He looks skeptical, his eyes shifting over to her and back to me, but eventually he nods, pressing the panic button firmly into my hand. "Don't put it in your purse, don't let go of it during the meal, and keep it out of sight."

I'm not sure exactly how I'm going to manage that, but I nod anyway. He's a little uptight, but this is his job.

Elizabeth sniffs again, pulling a tissue from her clutch and dabbing at her eyes. I'm a counselor, and I know this is my forte, but I hate when people cry. I don't know what to say or do. Especially in *this* situation, when I'm the person who put her son behind bars where he was then murdered.

We walk through the restaurant and the waitress leads us toward the back.

There are small, intimate tables placed throughout the main area with white tablecloths and vases of flowers. The ceiling consists of exposed beams and metal work, giving it a modern air. There are couples seated throughout, some lifting their gaze to us, but Elizabeth hurries past them all.

I'm sure she's gotten a lot of bad press lately with Landry's death and is worried about being recognized.

Phil follows closely behind me, scanning the open room, and when we reach the back wall he goes into the secluded dining area first to make sure it's clear before gesturing for me and Elizabeth to come in. He stands near the doorway and gives me a look, to which I squeeze the panic button in my hand and give him a small, reassuring nod.

Elizabeth goes to the coat rack in the corner and hangs her clutch there. She gestures to the table. "Sit down, love. Do you know what you'd like to eat?"

I take the seat facing the door, tucking the panic button under my leg in the seat so I can grab it if needed. I'm not sure it matters if Elizabeth sees the panic button or if Phil just doesn't want anyone getting nervous or wondering what it is, but I keep it hidden from her just in case.

Opening my menu, I glance over the top of it to see her looking back at me, her eyes still a lovely shade of dead.

I used to envy her blue eyes. They were bright crystals, aquamarines. The light from them is gone now, and I wonder if she lost it when Landry went to prison, or when he lost his life a few weeks ago.

"I'm not sure. I think I'll see what the waiter recommends," I say.

We make idle conversation as we wait for the waiter to come back to the table.

Elizabeth is curious about the bookstore and what I do there, and why I decided to get out of counseling. I wish I had a better reason to give her other than I just couldn't do it anymore. I wanted to help people, but I couldn't leave it at work. I wanted to dissect their brains and find out what made them tick, but when I had the information I didn't know what to do with it. I would lie awake at night, head spinning, anxiety throbbing, unsure how to help or what to do.

I remember a lifeguard from one summer when my mom used to take me to the community pool, making us kids swear if we saw another kid drowning we wouldn't jump in to try to save them. She'd said in their desperation they might drown us, too.

Somehow that never sunk in for me.

So while I'm still licensed and intend to stay that way, for now I'm going to keep running the bookstore and assessing people from afar. Maybe one day I'll go back to it. In the meantime, it's a helpful skill to have with best friends who are rape survivors and an ex-boyfriend's mother who's grieving.

Sixty-Four

Emmett

Red hair tangled and thrown halfway into a bun on the top of her head, eyes bleary and red, Lacey looks like a completely different person than she did just two days ago. I don't think she's slept at all. Gone is the delusional, air-headed party girl, and before me is a very pissed off inmate.

"You know, we could help you out of this situation if you just tell us what you know, Lacey," Alex tells her, tone low and gentle.

"You don't need to tell them anything because you didn't *do* anything," her lawyer parrots in her ear.

"I believe that you didn't do anything. I really do," Alex speaks again. "But I do think you know who's behind the attacks on Raven Jackson and Elliott James. I think you have information that could help us put the right person away for this. It's not fair that you're sitting in a cell and he's out in the world. Did you think he'd post bail for you? He hasn't. He's not going to. He doesn't care."

Lacey chuckles, the fire burning behind her eyes getting brighter.

"What's so funny?" I ask her, but she just shakes her head and keeps staring at her hands.

"What did he tell you, Lacey?" Alex asks. "Did he make you feel like you were special? A part of his family?

Are you scared of disappointing him? Look around. You're here and he's not. You're being held here while he gets off Scott free. That was his plan all along," he continues, all part of our plan to alienate Lacey from the attacker and then convince her to join *our family* and help *us* instead of *him*.

I can see her leg bouncing, faster and faster, like it's a measure of her frustration or annoyance at having to speak with us again. Or maybe we're getting to her.

Maybe it's working.

"Listen, Lacey, can I level with you for a second?" I ask.

Alex shoots me a warning look. I'm going off script.

"Sure," she responds flatly. The word is a challenge, one I'm going to rise to meet.

I pull out the chair across from her and sit down, looking her in the face, praying she can see the sincerity on mine. "I care deeply about Raven, and this case is personal for me. I know that doesn't matter much to you right now, but you are the key to unlocking this entire thing. Raven trusted you, Reggie trusted you, and you've broken that trust to join forces with someone who doesn't care about you. *They* do. Help us find who's behind this. Join our team, earn their trust back. Let's put this bastard behind bars and let them feel safe again. You have the power to do that. You know what he's planning and how to stop him."

I can almost feel Alex holding his breath, waiting for my words to sink in. She's a wildcard. Her bloodshot eyes meet mine, and again, I'm taken aback by the intensity and anger there. She holds my gaze for a second, two, three.

And then she starts laughing. Uncontrollably. Tears coming to her eyes.

Alex looks at me and I shrug, unsure what to do.

Lacey's lawyer throws his hands up, her cackles bouncing off the walls around us like a sickening melody.

And suddenly she stops.

The room is dead silent and it's eerie, and then she says, "Of course you assume it's a man."

Sixty-Five

Raven

"Would you like some wine?" The waiter is holding out a bottle and I nod, gesturing to my cup.

Elizabeth declines. I've never seen her decline wine.

Ordinarily I would question if that meant I shouldn't take some myself, if I was committing some high society faux pas by drinking what was offered and not requesting something more expensive; but the last five years have taught me to be firm in my decisions, so I stand by this one.

The waiter walks away, and I grab my glass, taking a gulp. We've danced around the subject long enough. A few more silent moments go by, and I can't stand it any longer.

"Elizabeth, are you all right?" I make sure my voice comes out as concerned as I feel. I want to make sure she's okay.

"Whatever do you mean, dear?" The 'dear' sounds a lot like a sob, but her face remains impassive.

"I'm sorry, forgive me. I know this is hard. Would you like to talk about him? Would that help?"

She cocks her head to the side, considering it. She's a strong woman, and snapping in public wouldn't be fitting to her high-class standards, but I'm praying she lets me in. We're in a room back here by ourselves. No one can see her if she does break down.

I slip into counselor mode.

"I think I would like that," she says, looking down at her lap, her voice unsteady and quiet.

"When was the last time you'd heard from him?" I go right for it but keep my tone gentle.

Maybe I can help her process some of these emotions, though I can't imagine she doesn't have a shrink in the city. With all the money they have, she probably has a team of them that come to her home.

"I visited him every weekend. Every Sunday. I had just seen him a few days before…you know." She coughs at the end to clear her throat, looking past me into nothing.

I look around for a tissue but don't see any. She pulls one out of her sleeve and dabs her eyes.

Now's my chance.

Just say it and get it out, Raven, so you won't have any regrets later.

I take a deep breath and say, "I just want you to know how sorry I am, really. I know that Landry and I ended on less than ideal terms, but I never intended for—"

We're interrupted by the shrill ringing of my cell phone in my purse, hanging from the coat rack. She looks startled, but nods at me to get it.

"I'm sorry, excuse me." I stand and walk over to it, giving her my back as I fumble through my purse to find my phone. It's Reggie. "Hello?"

"Raven!" I can hear sirens in the background, and he coughs before continuing. "I'm so sorry! The store is on fire, it's on fire! I'm out—" More coughing, and then, "I'm out. The fire department just got here. Mark and I are out front. You need to come back now!"

"Okay, okay, you're safe," I say, more for my own benefit than his. "Okay, it's all right. You're safe. The store…holy shit…I'm coming!" I hang up and spin around. "We have to go. My store is on fire, I have to go." I hear the panic in my own voice, but I'm calm. In shock maybe, but calm.

I grab my coat and my purse, turning to hand Elizabeth hers, but she's still sitting at the table, unmoving.

"Come on!" I'm frantic, trying to hand over her bag.

It takes me a moment to realize she's still not standing up.

She's not hurrying. She's not frantic.

She's…smiling.

Sixty-Six

Emmett

"It's a woman." It's a statement, not a question. My voice falls flat.

We never considered a woman was behind the entire scheme, mostly because of the rape. It's extremely uncommon for a woman to order a rape on another woman. Unless that wasn't her intention and the dirt-bag she hired to kidnap or harm Raven/Elli took that into his own hands.

Or maybe she's just that fucking evil.

The smile is back on Lacey's face. "Yes, it's a woman."

"Who, Lacey?" I ask, and I know the desperation in my voice is apparent.

She just smirks, folding her hands in front of her and looking at her lawyer. "I think I'm done here."

The door bursts open, Monica standing in the doorway. "We've got to roll. Poe's is on fire."

I'm running through the hallway, dodging officers and fumbling to dial Raven's number as I hear Lacey's cackling floating down the hallway.

Fuck.

Sixty-Seven

Raven

"What the fuck are you doing? Let's *go*!" I nearly yell.

Still that creepy smile, spread across her face. A shit eating grin if I've ever seen one.

I quickly realize I'm not leaving this room until this is handled, and I push the bookstore from my mind. I sit back down across from her, the panic button laying in the seat from when I had jumped up and abandoned it for my phone. I squeeze it in my hand, but I don't push the button yet. Any minute, Phil is going to burst in here after getting a call about the store.

"You took something from me. The only thing I ever wanted. The only person I ever loved," she says.

I start shaking my head. "I didn't take him from you, Elizabeth, he made that decision himself."

"No!" Her shriek makes my ears ring. "You, you little *whore*, you came from *nothing*. You *are* nothing. Your own father didn't want you. Your mother turned to drugs to escape you. You are *nothing*! And you took him from me!"

I stand, backing away from the table. "Elizabeth," I try to console her. I know the shock is all over my face. I've never heard her use this tone before.

I see the glint of silver and before I can think, I slam my thumb down on the panic button, just as she lifts the gun.

"You're going to pay for it. I took your store. There's nothing left now for anyone to remember you by. Your pride and joy, gone. Just like mine."

"I'm sorry that you feel that way, Mrs. Davis. I really am." *Deep breath, Raven. Calm, be calm.* "But I didn't do this." *Where the fuck is Phil?* I reach into my bag as slowly as I can, trying not to draw attention to myself as I grab my pistol.

The dead look in her eyes is gone, replaced by pure joy. *She's going to shoot me.*

My hand closes on the handle of my gun just as the door bursts open. I hear shots ring out and I fall to the ground, aiming and shooting as I fall.

Three shots ring out.

Two hit.

Phil rushes over to me. "Raven!" His hands are all over my body, looking for a wound.

"I think it's my shoulder, but I'm all right." I try to sit up and he helps me, grabbing my other arm. I don't feel anything, the adrenaline pumping too strongly through my body to register the pain.

I haven't let go of my gun, and it's still pointed toward her.

I make myself look, and there she is.

Slumped against the table, a puddle of red now staining the pristine white tablecloth. Her eyes open, now truly dead.

People are shouting. My ears are ringing.

I drop the gun.

The staff are rushing into the room. I can hear Phil telling them the area is secured. I hear sirens.

"Phil."

He bends down beside me, removing my jacket from my shoulder and trying to assess the wound but I shrug him off.

"My store."

Sixty-Eight

Emmett

"Somebody better update me *right fucking now*!"

"First, you need to calm down or you won't be any fucking help," Monica says, sneering at me, taking a curve in the road at ninety MPH as we rush to Raven's bookstore.

"She's not answering her phone. I don't think she's at the store. She should still be at dinner with…oh my fucking God."

We turn to each other at the same time and say, "Elizabeth."

"Fuck, fuck, *fuck*!" I slam my fist into the dashboard, dialing Phil for the tenth time. "Jesus Christ, answer the fucking phone!"

"Okay, calm down. She's probably fine. It may not be Elizabeth. For all we know she's enjoying a nice dinner and doesn't have her phone on her."

"Even so, the fucking bodyguard would have his!" I snap.

"That's true, but you need to go into this as the detective you are and get your head straight. We're going to find her. Someone is going to call. Let's just get to the shop and go from there."

I nod at her, bending over in my seat and putting my head between my hands, dialing Raven again. I thought when she was kidnapped I'd never have to experience that sort of panic again, but this is a hundred times worse. It goes to voicemail. Again.

Two minutes later we're pulling onto the block that Poe's is on, but we can't go any farther. Three firetrucks block the road, along with scattered police cars. The blue and red lights dance around the buildings, creating a light show.

I'm out of the car before Monica puts it in park, sprinting down the street with my badge out. No one stops me and asks; they all know.

I spot Reggie sitting on the curb across from the shop, wrapped in a blanket, soot on his face and tears streaming down his cheeks.

"Reggie."

He looks up as I reach him, and the tears start coming harder. "I'm so sorry. I tried to save it. I tried to grab it all, I just—"

"Where is Raven?"

He blinks up at me, confused. "She was at dinner with Elizabeth. She should be on her way. I called her and told her—"

"Have you heard from Phil?" I ask him.

"No, but Mark might have. He's giving his statement." He gestures to an ambulance sitting a little farther down the street.

I can't see him from here, there are not enough street lights and too many firefighters between us. "What happened?"

He takes a deep shaky breath, and coughs on the exhale. "I was up front, getting ready to close up. The last customer had just left. Mark was sitting by the front door, next to the windows. I was turning the computer system off when I heard the glass break. I thought someone had thrown a brick through the window and driven off, but it was something else. It was burning. And there were four of them, through two windows. Mark was cut up from the glass, but he was yelling for me to run to the back and get out. Everything happened so fast, I didn't have time to think about how to react. I grabbed the fire extinguisher but it wasn't enough. The sprinklers didn't come on. Everything was catching so quickly. I grabbed what I could and ran to the back, Mark following behind. We both needed oxygen but we're fine. He's being treated for the cuts from the glass. I think it's almost out now, but it's been burning for at least twenty minutes. You haven't heard from Raven?"

I shake my head.

My first concern is finding her and making sure she's safe, but I know seeing this store is going to devastate her.

Sixty-Nine

Raven

"I think I left my phone…in there."

Phil doesn't hesitate to say, "We'll get you a new one."

"Have you called him?"

"No, I'm going to now. I called Mark. He and Reggie made it out, and the fire department is there. I wanted to know the status of what was going on with your shoulder before I called Emmett." He looks sheepish, but I understand.

He doesn't want to scare Emmett without knowing the full extent.

Luckily, the bullet just grazed me, and they're bandaging me up now before we can leave and head to the shop. I've given my statement three times.

By some miracle, the restaurant had cameras in the dining areas, so they were able to pull the footage and review it along with mine and Phil's statements.

My head is spinning, but I can't even begin to process what's going on. "Someone also needs to call Elli. I'm sure this is on the news and she's going to be freaking the hell out."

He nods. "On it."

I watch as he calls Emmett, his relaxed stance going from timid to rigid in two seconds flat. I can hear Emmett yelling.

"Give me the phone," I instruct him.

"She wants to speak with y—" He shoves the phone in my hand and winces, mouthing 'sorry' as I bring it to my ear.

"Emmett," I start.

"Raven, holy shit. You're okay?"

"I'm all right, just shaken up. It's only a graze."

"What's just a graze?" The deadly calm in his voice even scares me a little, but I square my shoulders.

"Elizabeth shot me—"

"What?!"

"Let me tell you what happened before you start panicking."

"I'm sorry," he says, and I can tell he's trying to calm himself down. I imagine him pacing back and forth. "Please tell me."

"We were at dinner. I got the call from Reggie that the bookstore was on fire. When I tried to get her to come with me, she went into this whole spill about how I took her son away, blah blah, and then she pulled a gun out. I had already hit the panic button, and I had my gun. She shot at me and I shot as I was going down. Phil also shot as he was entering the room. I'm not sure who killed her, but she's dead. I don't want to talk about it. I just want to get out of here and get to my shop. Are you there?"

There's a pause on the other end of the line, like he's speechless. "Yes, I'm here now."

"And?" I ask.

"And it's pretty bad. But it's nothing you can't rebuild. Nothing *we* can't rebuild."

"I want you to go home," I tell him.

"What?"

"Go home. I'll call you tomorrow."

"Raven, I—"

"Go home, Emmett."

Seventy

Emmett

All the sounds of the firefighters, the chaos of everyone running around, and Reggie asking me what's wrong fades away as I realize Raven ended the call.

Go home? To my home? My apartment?

Not hers. Not the home she was referring to just the other night.

I take a look around, shrugging when my eyes land on Reggie. "I'm going to go," I tell him, knowing I sound as lost as I feel.

"Go where? What the fuck?" Reggie looks shocked.

"She asked me to go," I say under my breath, more to myself than to Reggie, my head spinning.

"Of fucking course she did. And you're going to listen to her?"

I look up, with what I'm sure is confusion showing on my face. "That's what she wants, that's what I'll give her."

"No. Absolutely not." He stands up from the curb, facing me. "This is what she does. Something is happening that is going to be emotionally hard for her to do deal with, and she doesn't want any witnesses around. That's how she functions. She doesn't trust anyone enough to see the ugly parts of her. If you leave now, you'll show her she's right not to trust you with her whole self."

I consider his words. "If I'm around when she gets here, she's going to kick my ass."

"Let her try," he tells me, with a smirk. "Fight back. That's her love language." He pats me on the shoulder and starts to walk back toward the store. "But if this is what you really want, if *she* is what you really want, you've got to break down those walls. Don't you dare leave."

A half hour later, Phil pulls up with Raven.

I'm talking to the fire chief, trying to get information on what or who caused the fire. We now know Elizabeth was behind it all, so we're assuming Brent Smallwood has made another appearance.

The cameras we had swiftly installed on the bookstore after the near kidnapping will hopefully give us a good look at the driver and make of the car, but we have to wait for the cloud footage to be pulled since the cameras were destroyed in the fire. Almost everything was.

Raven can't see me from where I'm standing, so I get an unfiltered view of her as she takes in the wreckage. Because the fire started in the front of the store, the entire front half is gone. Bricks are strewn around where the main structure was, and there's so much soot. Books that never got to tell their stories. Everything is still smoldering, so we're not allowed to sift through anything yet and probably won't be able to until tomorrow.

Phil pats her on her shoulder and goes over to speak with Mark, leaving her to assess it alone.

When she had first stepped out of the car, her shoulders were squared, back stiff and head high. Now that she thinks no one is watching, I see those shoulders sag a millimeter, not enough that anyone else would notice.

But I do.

I walk over, approaching her from behind.

"You didn't leave." She doesn't turn to face me, and I wonder how she knew it was me.

"No."

"I asked you to," she says.

"Yes."

"Why?" she asks flatly.

"Why did you ask, or why didn't I listen?"

She shrugs.

"You asked because you didn't think you could handle having me around for this. You didn't want me to see you break."

"And why didn't you listen?"

"Because not only do I want to be here when you break, I want to help you put yourself back together again."

Seventy-One

Raven

I turn to him then.

And it's not the strength in his voice. It's not so he can wipe the tears that are now streaming down my face. It's what he just said.

He wants to help *me* put *myself* back together, my bookstore back together.

He doesn't want to pick up the pieces himself. He wants to help me do it on my own. I could kiss him.

And I do.

I feel his arms circle my waist, and I don't care that there are still twenty firefighters on the street with us and my nostrils are filled with the smell of burnt paper. All that matters to me is this man in front of me. This man who sees me for who I am and what I need. This man who doesn't want to be my knight in shining armor, but my partner who wants to be here for support while I save myself.

He breaks the kiss and leans his forehead against mine. "Are you okay?"

I know what he's asking. I potentially killed someone today. My bookstore and my home are a pile of rubble behind us. "No, but I will be."

"Do you want to come back to my apartment? You can stay with me until it's all sorted out."

"Yeah, I'd like that. I need to call Elli and tell her what's going on."

"I already did. She should be here any second. I learned my lesson on keeping her in the dark."

I chuckle, burying my head in his chest and breathing in his clean scent. The only thread of sanity I have in this chaos.

"I know your walls have been up for a long, long time," he says, his voice deep and rough, with emotion.

I want to run on instinct, but I don't.

"I want to see all of the ugly parts of you. I want all of you, Raven Jackson. Forever. I know you don't need me, and I wouldn't change that. But I want inside those walls. You don't have to take them down, and I won't try to break them down. When you let me inside, I want it to be your choice, not because I forced my way in. But I'm here, I'm all in, ready when you are."

Another tear slips down my cheek and I almost laugh at the absurdity of this moment. I've spent my entire life feeling unwanted, forging a path of my own out of necessity. And this man, this perfect man, wants to share his life with me.

"I won't try to shut you out again. I promise. The walls will stay up. I'll work on that. And I can't promise anything, but you can come inside."

"I know you want to do things on your own, and you can. But you won't have to."

I give him a small nod, relief flooding through me. "I never want to do this again." I gesture around us but I know he knows what I mean. This last month. The fear, the insecurity, the danger. I never want to feel those things again. "I want to rebuild the store, rebuild my life, and leave all of this in the past. I don't want to feel the way she made me feel tonight ever again." I look off, down the road, remembering the harsh words Elizabeth spoke right before she tried to kill me. In a much smaller voice I admit, "I don't want to feel unwanted, ever again."

"You never will. We all have demons, Raven. And without them we wouldn't be who we are. But I promise, as long as I'm living, you'll never have to wonder if someone wants you."

"Nevermore," I say to him, with a grin. *Please get it. Please get it.*

"Nevermore," he replies, smirking back at me.

He's the one.

Epilogue

Raven

"Emmett." I nudge him, and he rolls over onto his stomach, thoroughly ignoring me and burying his head under the pillow.

I roll my eyes and take a second to appreciate the view, the one that never gets old.

Those back muscles flexing as his arms are under his head beneath the pillow. The tattoo scrawled across the underside of his right arm, matching the one written across my forearm. The same word that's engraved in our wedding bands: *Nevermore*.

"Wake up." I nudge him again, this time getting a groan in response. "The store opens in an hour. We need to go."

He finally rolls over, eyes squinting open and immediately landing on me. "Morning, gorgeous."

"Get your ass out of this bed, Emmett Fisher."

"Yes, wife."

But he doesn't get up. He grabs for me and I squeal, jumping off the bed and out of his reach. A grumble erupts from his chest and I feel my body heating at the sound.

"No, we do not have time for that. Get up!" I tell him.

I run into our attached master bath before he can jump up and grab me. I brush my hair and apply my makeup as quickly as possible because we really do have to leave in the next ten minutes.

We don't have the convenience of living above the shop anymore, but I'm in love with our home. A two-story farm house outside of town that we bought about six months ago and are slowly fixing up. We'll have more time to focus it on it now.

I open the bathroom door, half-expecting him to still be in bed, but he's not there. I rush down the steps, opening my mouth to yell for him, and stop short.

He's standing at the kitchen counter, iced coffee already in one hand for me, and a bouquet of daisies in the other. "Congratulations, gorgeous. You did it."

"*We* did it." I smirk, taking them both from him and getting on my tiptoes to press a kiss to his cheek. "Let's go."

We pull up in front of the shop. The outside looks almost exactly the same. The bricks that meet the sidewalk are blackened. I wanted to use them in the foundation of the new store. Something old and something new. The Poe's sign hangs proudly above the door, the same as before. But when we step inside, the similarities end.

"It takes my breath away," I say.

"*You* take my breath away."

I roll my eyes, swatting at him. "We really did it."

"We did."

In the last eight months, we've completely rebuilt and reimagined Poe's.

The inside still has the signature touches of Edgar Allen Poe, but everything is sleek and modern. White and black contrasts span every corner, the only color in the main room being the covers of the books that crowd the shelves. A fresh start.

I hear the thundering sound of expensive boots running down the stairs behind the new front desk and register.

"Rave?"

"It's us," I yell back.

Reggie pushes the hidden panel open and I grin. I couldn't leave it out.

"Todd!" he shouts over his shoulder. "It's go time!" He rushes over to me and gives me his classic bear hug. "I can't tell you how nice it is to not have to commute to work. No wonder you stayed as long as you did."

I laugh and let out a sigh, thankful that he and Todd agreed to move in upstairs so I could feel comfortable buying the house with Emmett. They were able to move in two weeks ago, and it's really helped having them here the majority of the time to get everything ready for the grand opening.

"You've already got a crowd out there," a voice says.

The bell above the door dings and I turn to see Elli waltzing in, looking like a million bucks—as always.

"How nice of you to show," I tease.

"Hey, I'm here, aren't I?"

I go to her and hug her. "Thank you for coming."

She squeezes me tighter and says, "I wouldn't miss it."

We've grown closer than ever over the last eight months, slipping back into our normal routine. With Elizabeth gone and Brent Smallwood behind bars, she's finally been able to get past her panic attacks and get mostly back to her former life. A decent percentage of the eligible men in town have helped her do so—but to each her own.

"Ready to open the doors? It's time." Reggie looks at me, excitement oozing from every inch of him. He's almost bouncing where he stands.

"Let's do it," I tell him.

He walks over to the double oak doors, opening them both wide and letting the fresh air in.

The first group to walk through the doors makes my heart swell with love. My dad, my two half-brothers, and my new stepmom walk over to me as they take in the store, pride beaming off all four of them.

I've always prided myself on getting through life without a family and doing it all on my own. But as I glance around at my new biological family, Reggie and Todd, Phil and Mark who are coming through the door now, Elli who's flirting with one of the authors who's setting up to do a signing today, one handsome Marine that has a familiar grin (the other still deployed, but had sent his love to us last night via Facetime), and last but not least Emmett, who's smiling back at me, I realize they've been here all along. Pieces of my soul scattered about for me to find.

And although it was a wild ride, I'm thankful for every second of it—because it brought me these people.

The walls are down.

Nevermore.

Acknowledgments

The fact that I'm writing acknowledgments for an actual novel that I actually wrote...I officially can't even.

To my husband, thank you for always being the eight to my nine. I love you. Thank you for supporting me and my dreams. Always.

For my girls, being your mama is my favorite thing in the world. I can't wait to watch you all grow up and be your own heroines.

To my dad, thank you. For the *Barnes and Noble* trips, Coke Icees, and everything in between.

For my family, I love you. Jordan, Cam, Kenzie, Patti and Rick, Nana and Papa, Angela, all of my in-laws. All of you. Thank you.

Especially Mollie. Thank you for being the perfect bonus mom, and for all the things you do for us. Also for giving birth to my soulmate. I owe you one.

My squad. My girls. I am so thankful for all of you. Haley, Alicia, Stacey (both of you), Jilly, Cam, Jessica, Lisa, Lorena, Trina, Carrie and the LitChicks. So many more. I'm forever grateful for you.

My BOMB editor (how many times have I said that now?), Christina Hart. You're a saint and the best professional hype woman.

Kat Savage for this amazing cover. It's perfect. You're a genius.

Every English teacher I've ever had, thank you for keeping the love of literature and writing alive. Mrs. Wilson, Ms. Barrier, Mrs. Rutledge, I'm looking at you.

Wrenn's Warriors, and everyone who's supported me in this wild and random journey, thank you.

Edgar Allen Poe, you genius, you. Thank you for sharing your madness with us.

And anyone I've left out, you know I'm a nine. I'm forgetful, and I'll lose sleep over wondering who I didn't list, so accept this as your acknowledgment. *Please?*

I love you all.

Here's to the first of many, many more.

About the Author

Wrenn Montgomery resides in North Carolina with her husband and three daughters. She spends her time psychoanalyzing strangers and writing about them in steamy romances.

Low-key stalking approved

Instagram: @wrennmontgomery
Facebook: @authorwrennmontgomery
Facebook Reader Group: http://bit.ly/WrennsWarriors
Goodreads: http://bit.ly/GRWrennMontgomery
Email: WrennMontgomery@gmail.com

Made in the USA
Middletown, DE
06 January 2020